# Master
## An *Impossible* Novel

By Julia Sykes

D1520060

For everyone who read *Mentor* and asked for more
Master and Kathy.

# *Impossible* Series Reading Order

While the books in the *Impossible* series can be read as standalone romances, the following is the chronological order of the stories:

*Impossible: The Original Trilogy (Monster, Traitor, and Avenger)*
*Savior* (An *Impossible* Novel)
*Rogue* (An *Impossible* Novel)
*Knight* (An *Impossible* Novel)
*Mentor* (An *Impossible* Novella)
*Master* (An *Impossible* Novel)

Please note that *Master* is directly connected to *Knight* and *Mentor*. It is not necessary to read those books before reading *Master* in order to follow the story, but it will enhance the reading experience.

# Chapter 1

## *Katie*

*I'll be watching you today. And every day, until I finally take you. Don't worry, Kathy. I don't want to break you. But I do want to make you scream. I want to make you mine. Come and find me. Come to me, pet.*

My stomach began to churn before my mind could fully process the words. It was as though they stared up at me from the dirty scrap of paper they were scrawled upon, as though the eyes of the person who had written them were piercing my soul. I felt violated, dirty. The wash of horror made my throat convulse as bile rose. How could nothing more than ink on a page affect me so viscerally?

It could, because the intent behind those words was so abhorrent that it made me want to lash out at my invisible assailant like a wild, cornered animal. But there was no assailant, and my adrenaline burned through my veins, scorching them when it found no outlet.

"Katie? You okay?"

I whirled, and my fist swung in a practiced arc. In the half a heartbeat it took for me to register the familiar voice, I managed to slow the punch. My hesitation gave my partner the split second of warning he needed to catch my wrist, blocking the hit.

"Whoa, Sparrow. What's got your panties in a twist?"

"Dex. Don't sneak up on me like that." It was much easier to turn my fear into ire, even if it wasn't warranted.

He gave me a small frown, and he didn't release my wrist. He lowered it so that it hung at his side, almost as though he was holding my hand. "I wasn't sneaking. I said your name three times before you tried to pop me across the jaw." His fingers squeezed in reprimand. "Thanks for changing your mind at the last second there."

All the aggression left me on a heavy sigh. I ran my hand through my hair. The familiar weight of the copper curls was comforting, as was the little tug on my scalp as I pulled on the strands. The sensation helped ground me, tethering me to the moment so that I could leave my fear behind.

"Sorry. I'm just tired, that's all." I didn't want to tell Dex about the note. He would just freak out and go all alpha male protective on me, as though I was one of the victims we worked with all too often. I wasn't a victim. As a member of the Violent Crimes Task Force for the FBI, I was the hunter, the one who put away the bastards who turned those poor women into victims.

I shifted my body to place myself firmly between Dex and the evidence. His frown deepened, drawing his masculine features down into something forbidding, if no less handsome. Pale blue eyes shot through with navy glared down at me, and the way the light caught his close-cropped blond hair made him look like an avenging angel. I couldn't deny that Dex was intimidating when he got like this. It was one of the reasons why he was such a good FBI agent.

"Don't lie to me, Sparrow. I can always tell. What's bothering you?" Dexter Scott, human lie detector. Another quality that made him a good agent. And a pain in my ass.

My sigh was one of annoyance this time. "Don't call me that. I get it. My surname sounds like 'bird.' I don't like the cutesy nicknames at the office. I'm an agent, just like you."

His fingers squeezed my wrist again. "Okay, then, *Agent Byrd.* What's really bothering you?"

"Has it ever occurred to you that if I'm being evasive, it means I don't want to share? Social niceties dictate that you back off."

Even the casual shrug of Dex's shoulders was intimidating. The movement called attention to his imposing stature. At five foot eight, I don't consider myself short, but when being stared down by a six foot four, heavily muscled god of a man, I felt as small as a child.

"No." He informed me. "Tell me what's going on with you, Sparrow."

It was no longer a friendly question. It was an order. Dex didn't outrank me, but I found myself cracking anyway. My body shifted, and my eyes cut to my desk, where the note lay on my keyboard. From a distance, it didn't look like anything more than a scrap of paper, but I could feel malevolence rolling off it.

Dex's long fingers snatched it up.

"Don't!" I protested, but his eyes were already scanning the sickening words. In the five seconds it took him to read it, his features twisted from disapproval to rage.

His eyes were twin blue flames when they found mine. "Who sent this?"

"I don't know. I just found the envelope in my box. It's probably not even for me. It might be evidence from a case someone didn't label properly. It's addressed to Kathy, not Katie."

Dex's hard expression told me I was being willfully ignorant. "Kathy can be short for Katherine. Don't pretend like you don't know it's for you."

"I don't know that," I snapped to cover the fact that I suspected he was right. I couldn't show weakness. Not at the office. Not ever. "Like I said, it could be mislabeled evidence. I'll see if I can track down what happened. You shouldn't be touching that without gloves."

"Well, it's too late for that now. We'll have to take into account the fact that you and I touched it when we run it for prints."

"Thank you for being sensible." Relief sank into me at his agreement that the note had nothing to do with me personally. "I'll just take this to the lab and-"

"Not yet, you won't," Dex cut over me. "We're showing this to Frank."

"Why? It's part of one of my cases. He doesn't need to-"

This time he stopped me with a low growl. His fingers tightened around my wrist again. "I already told you to stop pretending. We both know this is a personal threat, Katie. And I'm not letting you bury it just because you're scared."

"I'm not scared!" I insisted. I couldn't let him see that I *was* scared, even if he was my best friend. "You're just being unreasonable."

"You're lying again." It was a cool statement of fact.

I tugged against his hold on my wrist. He didn't even seem to notice. "Just leave it, okay? Even if it is for me, it needs to be processed just like any other piece of evidence. Let me take it to the lab. I can deal with this." I was reassuring myself just as much as I was trying to persuade him of that fact.

"I know you can deal with it, but that doesn't mean you have to do it on your own. It's okay to be scared, Katie. This is some scary shit. And that's why I'm not going to let you quietly try to handle it by yourself."

"You're not going to *let* me?" That truly got my hackles up. I didn't usually mind my friend's pushiness, but right now, with my emotions fraying, I couldn't face it. "Careful, Dex. Your alpha-douche is showing."

To my surprise, he chuckled darkly. "Oh, Sparrow, you haven't even glimpsed my 'alpha-douche.' I can assure you, he would most certainly *not* appreciate that title."

I shifted uncomfortably. His touch on my wrist suddenly burned much hotter. My eyes slid away from his. "Damn it, Dex," I muttered, my confident façade cracking ever so slightly. "Don't make this a big deal. Please."

"I'm not making it a big deal. This is serious, Katie. You're going to talk to Frank about it, and you're going to keep me updated. Don't keep things like this from me. I won't let anything happen to you."

I glanced up at him and saw a hint of fear for me flash through the righteous anger in his eyes. That swayed me more than his demands. My partner cared about me.

"I wouldn't let anything happen to you, either, Dex," I admitted. "Thanks for looking out for me."

The taut lines around his full mouth softened. "Always."

A long moment passed between us, and I felt that the weight of his stare was more significant than just concern for my safety. There was something else there. It was answered by a stirring of affection deep within me.

"I'll take the note to Frank, then," I finally broke the intense silence.

"Good." Dex's voice was a touch deeper than usual as he delivered his approval. It made me feel warm inside, and I gave him a small smile as I took the piece of paper back from him. It wasn't as scary now that my partner shared the burden of its contents.

Well, it had gone from terrifying to mildly horrifying on the fear-inducing scale. But at least now I could touch it without feeling like vomiting.

Dex finally released my wrist. "Go on, then." The upward curve of his lips was softly encouraging.

I nodded. "I'll let you know how it goes." With that, I skirted around him before my courage failed me. Trepidation and a touch of shame bled into the sense of calm I had found with Dex. Not only was I worried about Frank's reaction to the note, but I was also embarrassed to show him such an overtly sexual threat. Franklin Dawes might be my boss, but he was also a father figure to me. What girl wants to discuss something like this with her dad?

I shook my head. Frank might have known me since I was a teenager, but I wasn't a girl any longer. And my real father was dead in the ground, along with my mother. I had never known her, but I had lost Dad when I was seventeen. Frank – Dad's partner and one of his closest friends – had helped fill that gap. He had even helped guide me to my job with the Bureau. I had faced some heinous crimes with him, but none of them had ever involved me personally.

Even though I held it gingerly between my thumb and forefinger, the paper seemed to burn them by the time I knocked on Frank's office door.

"Come in." His voice was deep and calm, as always. Frank never lost that sense of composed control, no matter what crime we faced. He was an incredibly strong man, emotionally as well as physically. Even if he was a touch stern, I always felt safe around him. His consistent moods made his supportive presence incredibly comforting, and they gave me the strength I needed to match that calm control when it came to facing the sick criminals I hunted.

Focusing on that knowledge, I took a deep breath and stepped into his office.

His face lit up when I entered. "Katie," he beamed. He always had that warm smile for me. It was the only time I ever saw his cool demeanor melt. It made me feel special, cared for. The faint crow's feet around his polished mahogany eyes deepened, and his perfect white teeth flashed.

Frank cared about me. He would help me through this.

"What can I do for you?" He asked genially.

"This…" I fumbled. "This was waiting for me when I came back in this afternoon." I dropped the note so quickly that it fluttered through the air for a second before landing on the desk in front of him.

He reached for his gold wire framed reading glasses and lifted the paper closer to his eyes. His brows rose nearly all the way to his meticulously-styled steel grey hair. After a moment, his expression went carefully blank, and his gaze returned to me. Tension gripped my muscles at the sight of it. The warmth he usually afforded me was gone, as was his usual calm. It was as though it was taking all his effort to conceal his emotions.

"Who sent this?" His voice was softer than I had ever heard it.

"I... I don't know. It was in an envelope in my box when I went to check it just now."

Frank placed it carefully on his desk. "We'll run it for prints. Has anyone else touched it other than you and me?"

"Dex. He held it."

His lips thinned in disapproval. "I'll make sure no one else does. I'll personally deliver it to the lab."

"I can handle it," I insisted quickly. I hated how upset Frank seemed over the situation, and I didn't want him to think I couldn't deal with the note. I didn't want him to think I was afraid. "I'll take it-"

"I didn't ask for your permission," he cut me off. I swallowed hard and took a step back. I had seen this domineering side of him before, but he never turned it on me. He sighed, and his expression softened to something more soothing. "I'll take care of this, Katie."

The paternal light in his eyes let me know the unspoken significance of those words: *Let me take care of you.*

The offer was too tempting to refuse. It was all I could do to stop myself from throwing myself in his arms and seeking his comfort, as I had done so many times after my father passed away.

I blinked hard to clear the tears that glossed over my deep green eyes. "Thanks, Frank."

"I'm very proud of you for being so brave about this, Katie," he told me kindly. "But this is serious, and you shouldn't deal with it on your own."

"That's what Dex said. He convinced me to show you the note."

"You should have come to me immediately." His voice sharpened, and just like that, I felt like a chided child.

"I know," I mumbled, dropping my eyes.

"You will tell me the next time something like this happens. Before you consult with anyone else. You're my responsibility, Katie. I won't let anyone hurt you."

It was the same thing Dex had said. He wasn't the only alpha male in the office. Frank's insistent protectiveness didn't grate on me the way my partner's had, though. If anything, the fatherly instinct to keep me safe was gratifying.

"I promise I'll come to you first."

"Good." Frank nodded once, satisfied. "Now, there's something else I need to discuss with you. One of the guys from the New York unit is coming in to work with you on The Mentor case."

*The Mentor.* I suppressed a shudder at the name. Well, the man I was hunting didn't have a name. He didn't have a face, either. Not yet. But I was determined to identify him. If he was anything like his mentee – Carl Martel – he had likely abducted, raped, and killed dozens of women.

"Why?" I asked to distract myself from the images of battered women that raced across my mind. "Why am I not working with Dex?"

Frank's lips twisted in distaste. He was obviously as unhappy with the assignment as I was. "Kennedy Carver – the New York unit director – suggested it. Martel's last victim, Lydia Chase, was selected because of her interest in the BDSM lifestyle. Carver thought it would be helpful if someone with experience in that area was on hand to help here in Chicago."

Martel had lived outside New York City, but Lydia Chase had been abducted from Chicago, so members of both units were searching for The Mentor. I nodded my agreement with the new agent's assignment to our field office. We could use all the help we could get.

"Who's the agent?" I asked.

"His name's Reed Miller. He's a rookie, barely four months with the Bureau. But Carver insists he's experienced in the BDSM lifestyle and has done good work so far." Frank's frown deepened. "I want you to watch yourself around him, Katie. Professionally, I approve of his partnership with you. But he's new, and I don't know if I trust him with your safety. Be careful."

"I will be," I promised. "If Carver says he's good, I'm sure he'll have my back."

*Although I wish I could keep Dex at my back.* I knew my current partner, and I trusted him with my life. Being paired with a stranger didn't sit entirely well with me.

A knock at the door distracted me. Frank glanced past me to look through the glass wall at the front of his office. The blinds were open, revealing the man who stood just outside.

"Come in." Frank's tone lacked the warmth it held when he invited me in.

The man who stepped through the door wasn't just a rookie; he was probably around my age. I hadn't expected to be partnered with someone so young. Or so breathtakingly gorgeous. The man was as tall as Dex, but where my partner was all light and righteousness, Reed Miller was dark and positively sinful. His skin was golden, and his black hair matched his eyes. They were dark, fathomless pools. A woman could drown in those eyes.

"Katie, this is Reed Miller. Miller, this is your new partner, Agent Katherine Byrd."

"It's so nice to finally meet you, Agent Byrd. I've heard great things." His voice was as sensual as the lips from which it issued.

Automatically, I reached my hand out to shake his, and strong heat enveloped my fingers. It raced up my arm, flooding my chest before finding its way down lower in my abdomen. The warmth pooled somewhere entirely unprofessional.

*"Be careful."* Frank's warning echoed in my mind.

Oh, I was going to have to be very careful when it came to Reed Miller.

# Chapter 2

"Agent Miller. It's nice to meet you, too." My voice was a touch breathier than usual. I shot an uneasy glance at Frank as I withdrew my hand. What girl wants her dad to see her getting the hots for a guy?

*I am not a little girl anymore.* I hadn't been for a long time. When I had wanted to break down and hide from the world like a child after my father's death, Frank had been the one to drag me out. He had helped me become strong. He had helped me become a woman.

But the disapproving slant of his lips made me want to run to my room and pull my bedcovers over my head. Frank had helped me grow up, but he still had the unique ability to make me feel like a stupid little girl when he turned that particular frown on me.

"You two should go compare notes." Frank's voice was positively chilly, a clear dismissal. "I want you to find The Mentor soon, Katie. Don't get distracted."

*Distracted.* His meaning was obvious. He had noticed my instant physical attraction to Reed. I dropped my eyes as my embarrassment doubled. "Of course, sir."

"And I'll take this note to the lab. Come to me immediately if anything else happens."

The reminder of the sickening threat just twisted the knife Frank had stuck into my gut. Dads sucked sometimes. I much preferred his comforting hugs to his shame-inducing admonishments.

"Yes, sir." My meek answer was all I had to offer.

"Go on, then. Report back to me with any new developments."

"Yes, sir." This time it was Reed who answered.

I met Frank's hard eyes one last time before turning from him. A strange mixture of defeat and determination filled me at the sight of his disapproval. I had let him down, but I would do better next time. I would catch The Mentor and make him proud.

"So the boss is a hard ass," Reed remarked as soon as the door closed behind us. "I'm used to that with my boss, Kennedy. Don't let it get you down."

I glared up at him. He didn't know the first thing about my relationship with Frank. "Don't you dare say anything against Frank. He's the best man I know."

Reed's hands raised in a placating gesture. "Whoa, I didn't say he was a bad guy. I have nothing but respect for Kennedy. He's a great unit director. That doesn't mean he's not a hard ass. If anything, that's why he's good at his job." He shook his head and grinned at me. "This isn't how I wanted to start our relationship, Katie. I can call you, Katie, can't I?"

I just nodded, temporarily struck dumb by his dazzling smile. I think I would have agreed to anything in the wake of that devilish grin.

*"Be careful."* Frank's warning played through my mind.

"The boss decrees that we compare notes. Could I interest you in doing that over coffee?"

I shook my head. "I don't do coffee. I'm an iced tea girl." The small smile on my face felt strange. Was it flirty? The very idea was shocking. I had only ever had one real relationship, and that lasted all of two months. I secretly suspected that Frank had run George off, but I was grateful for that, really. I had already been getting bored of him.

I realized I was staring into Reed's eyes with inappropriate intensity. Those black pools were just far too fascinating. Their inky depths held secrets. Sensual secrets. I had never known attraction like this. To be honest, it was a bit scary. But not scary enough to make me look away.

Those eyes widened in dramatic shock. "Are you sure you're an FBI agent?" He asked, a smile playing around the corners of his far-too-sexy mouth. "Shouldn't you have an IV drip with black coffee like the rest of us?"

I made a show of peeking around his large body. "I don't see an IV bag trailing along after you."

"Hence my desperate need for a coffee fix." His shudder was exaggerated. I wasn't the only one flirting. The concept that this gorgeous man was interested in me was almost jarring. Men never paid any attention to me. Well, with the exception of the scumbags I arrested. They always had a lewd remark to toss my way.

My smirk widened to an almost silly grin. I felt like a teenager spotting her first crush. I seemed to be having a lot of flashbacks today. Only, the butterflies Reed awoke in my stomach were decidedly nicer than the uneasy churning sensation elicited by Frank's disapproval.

"Well, I wouldn't dream of making you go into withdrawals," I said lightly. "Let me grab my keys and we'll go."

"Thank you." Reed's sigh of relief was comical in its intensity.

"Katie. Who's this?" Dex's deep voice cracked through the little bubble of giddiness that had engulfed me. Suddenly, his heat was beside me. He was very obviously in my personal space, and he was glaring at Reed.

*Whoa.* That stony stare was usually reserved for criminals in interrogation.

*"What's wrong with you?"* The furrow between my brows communicated my silent question. Dex and I were close enough that we could often express ourselves without words. It was immensely valuable on a stakeout.

Dex didn't even acknowledge me. His blue eyes positively crackled as they fixed on Reed's.

Reed, on the other hand, appeared coolly implacable, completely unaffected by my imposing partner's overtly aggressive stance. If I didn't know better, I would say Dex was being… territorial.

Shit. He wasn't going to take the news that I had a new partner well at all.

"Reed, this is Dexter Scott. Dex, this is-"

"Reed Miller," Reed interrupted me and extended his hand. "I'm Katie's new partner."

Dex's eyes flashed, but he grasped Reed's hand in greeting. Only, he held on a few seconds too long, and I noticed both of the men's knuckles whiten as they each tightened their grips.

"Dex." I said his name sharply to put an end to the inexplicable alpha-off. I suppressed the urge to roll my eyes.

*Another alpha male in the office. Great.* My inner voice dripped with sarcasm.

"Believe me, I didn't ask for a new partner. You know I wouldn't do that." My voice softened, urging him to believe me. I might not hate my new assignment – I wouldn't mind looking at Reed every day – but I truly did regret losing my friend at my back. Especially after seeing how much it hurt him. I knew him well enough to recognize that his macho aggression was just that: an effort to mask his hurt. He didn't want to lose sight of me any more than I wanted to stop protecting him.

My fingers rested on his forearm. I could feel the tension in it from his efforts to crush Reed's hand. Reed appeared completely unfazed.

"This was Frank's call," I told Dex gently.

My touch was all it took to call him back to me. His eyes still blazed when they met mine, but I resolutely held his stare. His lips pressed into a harsh slash, but he released Reed.

"You're going to keep me updated on the case," Dex ordered, his eyes burning his will into me. He pinned me there, waiting for my compliance.

"Okay, Dex." His name was a promise.

He nodded once, but he was far from satisfied. "I don't like this. Especially after that note you received. I don't want to let you out of my sight." The look he shot at Reed when he spoke was one of warning. "I'm going to talk to Frank about this."

With that, he turned on his heel and stalked towards our boss' office. I winced.

*Time to go.* I didn't want to be here when the bomb went off. Frank and Dex going head to head wasn't going to be pleasant, and, seeing as I was the cause of the conflict, I wanted to be far away from the building when it started.

"Let's get that coffee," I told Reed over my shoulder. I was already striding toward my desk to grab my keys.

"What note?" He asked, keeping pace with me. "Franklin and Dexter both mentioned it."

"Don't let Dex hear you using his full name. He hates it."

"I'm pretty sure he already doesn't like me," Reed remarked.

"Well, calling him Dexter will make it worse." I only just stopped myself from explaining that the other kids had bullied him by calling him Poindexter when he was in elementary school. He was very touchy about his glasses, and I was one of the only people who had ever seen him in anything but contacts. I got the feeling my friend wouldn't appreciate me sharing something so personal with a man he obviously disliked.

"You didn't answer me," Reed admonished. "What note?"

"I'll tell you about it later," I deflected. I *so* wasn't ready for another man to go all alpha protective on me in the space of half an hour. Their concern only made it that much more difficult to mask my fear. "Let's get out of here before the explosion, okay?" I could already hear Dex's furious voice floating through the glass wall of Frank's office. My pace quickened.

I practically rocked back and forth on the balls of my feet on the long elevator ride down to the parking garage. I couldn't get out of there fast enough. If Dex decided to come back to argue more, Reed might end up with a black eye. My partner was fierce, but I had never seen him turn this side of himself against another agent. He must really be upset about losing me to act so uncharacteristically vicious.

I suddenly felt guilty for my moment of excitement at Reed's proximity. It felt like a betrayal. I edged away from him and his nearly irresistible magnetism as soon as we exited the elevator. His scent – rich and salty, like masculine musk caught on a tropical ocean breeze – filled the small space. It was as tempting to breathe in as it was to drown in his dark eyes. Everything about the man exuded sexuality. I wondered if everyone could see it, or if it just affected me in particular. Glancing over at his perfect profile, I decided any woman would swoon over him.

*Pull yourself together, Byrd.*

I had a sadistic serial killer to catch. I most certainly didn't have the time or brain power to waste ogling my new partner. It was a disservice to the women who had suffered at The Mentor's hands. He might be torturing some poor woman right now, and there was nothing I could do to stop him. Not yet.

That thought helped me gather my resolve. How could I lust after a near-stranger – and a coworker, no less – when the faceless woman might be desperately hoping for me to come to her rescue? My sexual interest in Reed was effectively doused.

My usual calm didn't return until I was in my car and pulling away from the potential disaster that was occurring in my boss' office, fourteen floors above the garage. Then Reed went and obliterated it again.

"So why was I brought in on this case?" He sounded genuinely confused.

I cut my eyes over to him where he sat in the passenger seat. We had already been over this. "I thought Frank and Kennedy discussed this with you. You're…" I stumbled over the words. Knowing them and saying them aloud in a matter-of-fact tone were completely different things. "You're in the BDSM lifestyle, and they thought it would be helpful to have you in the Chicago office."

Reed still appeared puzzled. "But you have Dex here. Why would you need me?"

"What do you mean? What does Dex have to do with this?"

"He's a Dom."

I blinked. "What?"

"A Dominant," Reed explained.

"I know what a Dom is. I've been researching for this case. But you don't know what you're talking about. Dex isn't involved with that. I would know." I shuddered at the thought of my friend being into BDSM.

"What was that?" Reed asked sharply.

"What was what?"

"That look of disgust. Does the idea of Dex being in the lifestyle bother you?"

I shook my head. "You're wrong about that. Dex would never hurt a woman."

"And you think I would?" The easygoing man who had so coolly met Dex's challenge was suddenly coldly furious. "Is that what you think of me? That I abuse women?"

"Of course not!" It had never even crossed my mind that Reed would be capable of such a thing. But that's what BDSM was about…

"You're lying. You think I'm like Carl Martel. You think I'm like The Mentor. Don't you?"

"No!"

"Then why does the idea of Dex being a Dom bother you?" He demanded.

"It's just… I didn't mind the idea of BDSM," I confessed. "But then I talked to Lydia Chase. I saw the photos of the marks Martel left on her…" My stomach turned at the memory of the lacerations left by the whip, of the dead look in Lydia's eyes when she was first found by Agent Smith James in New York. Martel had chosen her because of her interest in BDSM. All of that had happened to her because she liked pain with sex.

"And you think Martel was a Dominant?"

"No!" I insisted again. Reed was backing me into a corner. It was so much easier to be repulsed by what had happened to Lydia than facing my own interest in being tied down during sex. "I know he was a sick psychopath. I don't think you're like him at all."

"Then why does the idea of Dex being a Dom bother you?" He prompted again.

*Because I can't reconcile the man I care about so deeply with the harsh discipline of BDSM. Especially not when it makes me hot just thinking about it.*

I knew my pale skin had turned bright red with my blush. "It just does," I replied lamely.

"You're interested in BDSM." Reed's cool conclusion made my stomach drop.

"I am not!" My denial sounded desperate in my own ears.

"Don't do that."

"Do what?"

"Lie to me. I won't tolerate it."

"You won't *tolerate* it?" I had gone from desperate to indignant. Again, I found myself feeling like a child. The man was throwing me for a loop.

"No. I won't. You're lying to me, and you're lying to yourself. We're partners, and we have to be completely honest with one another. I have to know I can trust you."

My cheeks flamed impossibly hotter. Reed had effectively chastised me. Of course he needed to trust me. He wasn't dressing me down to force me to accept my secret desires; he was ensuring I would have his back if shit hit the fan.

I took in a deep breath and blew it out slowly. "You can trust me. I promise."

He nodded. "Good. Then you'll tell me about this note now." It wasn't a question.

"That has nothing to do with The Mentor case. It's private." I wasn't ready to talk to Reed about the threat. The sexual connotations of the note and the words about making me scream paralleled too closely with our tense discussion of my discomfort about BDSM. I wasn't ready to divulge its contents to my new partner.

"It's not private. Not from me."

"Why?" I snapped, irritated. "Because you're a Dom, you think you have the right to bully me about everything in my life?"

"No. I have a right to know if you're in danger because I'm your partner. If you're in the line of fire, then I am, too."

Again, he was so reasonable. I was making this all about me. I was making this all about *sex*. Yes, sexual abuse was at the heart of this investigation, as was BDSM, but that didn't mean that all of Reed's comments were about my personal sexuality. He had every right to know if there was a threat lurking behind me. He was right; it would put him in danger, too.

"Okay," I allowed. "I received a note today. A threat. Well, Dex and Frank are convinced it's a threat. I think it's mislabeled evidence from one of my cases."

"You're lying again, Katie." Reed's voice was quiet, a gentle admonition. "Tell me what the note said."

"It said…" I swallowed. "It said someone's watching me. He wants to hurt me. He… He said he wants to make me *his*."

*But I do want to make you scream. I want to make you mine. Come and find me. Come to me, pet.* I told Reed the general gist of the note, but every vile word was burned into my brain. I didn't think I would ever be able to get them out.

# Chapter 3

I was trembling by the time I finished telling him the contents of the note. Somehow, admitting them aloud made the threat more real. The disgusting words hung in the air between us for a moment, tainting the space around me. I chanced a glance over at Reed. He was stiff with suppressed anger.

"Please, don't." I had to cut him off before he could start. "Don't go all alpha-protective on me. I've had enough of that from Dex and Frank. I can deal with this."

"Katie." My name was sharp with disapproval and his own anger towards the man who had sent the note. "Don't pretend like this is nothing."

"Please. You're making it worse. Frank's taking the note to the lab for biometric analysis. There's nothing more we can do about it. Just leave it. We need to focus on catching The Mentor. He's more important."

"Your safety is important."

I stayed focused on parallel parking, but Reed's stare burned into my cheek.

"Not as important as stopping The Mentor. He might be torturing a woman right now, and I'm going to be sipping iced tea. I'm fine."

A long moment of heavy silence passed before Reed sighed. "Okay, Katie. We can focus on the case. But don't think I'm going to drop this. We're going to follow up on it."

"I've put dozens of sickos away, Reed. It's probably one of them, and they've found a way to get the message to me. They're all behind bars. I'm not in danger. Please respect that I can handle this."

To my surprise, Reed shot me a wry smile.

"What?" I asked, uncomfortable that I wasn't in on the joke.

"You remind me of Sharon, my partner at the New York field office. She gets really prickly if I question her competence at her job, too." His expression turned more serious. "Of course I respect you, Katie. You wouldn't have been assigned to The Mentor case if you weren't good at what you do. But that doesn't mean I'm not going to look out for you. That's my job."

He was so rational. It was impossible to stay snappish when he laid everything out so calmly. It was comforting. I was suddenly happy to have Reed at my side for more reasons than just his physical beauty.

"Okay," I conceded. "Thanks, Reed."

It was the best I could hope for. If Reed was anything like Dex and Frank – and it was becoming more apparent that he was with every passing minute – he wasn't going to stop trying to find the man who threatened me.

*Dex and Frank are bossy like him. Does that really mean Dex is a Dom? What about Frank?*

I couldn't handle thinking about my father figure like that. It was too weird to contemplate his sexual preferences for even a moment. I shook my head. This case was definitely getting to me. I would start seeing Doms everywhere if I went on like this.

"Come on," I said as lightly as I could manage. "Let's get you that coffee before you get the shakes."

The perfect grin he shot me knocked all my worries from my brain, and I found myself inexplicably smiling back at him. The stern side of Reed was all business, but when he turned his lighter side on me, I couldn't help being charmed. More like stunned, really.

It took us a good fifteen minutes to walk from the parking spot I had found to Starbucks. The sky had darkened to indigo, and the breathtaking lights of the Chicago skyline surrounded us.

Under other circumstances, Reed and I might have been one of the couples strolling out on their date nights. Unfortunately, my Friday night consisted of discussions about sadistic murderers. Not exactly romantic dinner conversation.

Also unfortunate was the good foot of space between Reed and me. Even with that distance, I could feel his heat at my side. My hand burned to reach out for his. The desire to touch him was almost overwhelming.

*Stop that!* Reed was my partner, not my date. No matter how beautiful or how impossibly alluring he was, he was most definitely off-limits. Furthermore, he was definitely unattainable. I was decidedly unfeminine; I didn't wear skirts or even makeup. And I knew how to throw a punch. Men weren't interested in me, much less sensual gods like the man who walked beside me.

No, he didn't walk. He prowled. His every movement was carefully controlled, as graceful as a stalking panther.

It was almost a relief when we sat down with our drinks. At least there was a table separating me from Reed. I would be able to think more clearly. About The Mentor.

The Mentor was enough to make the last of the heat between us evaporate. It was impossible to think about anything remotely arousing when focusing on that sick bastard. I took a sip of my tea to counteract the sudden dryness in my mouth.

"So, tell me what you know about Carl Martel. What have you guys found in New York?"

Reed grimaced over his coffee cup at the name. "Unfortunately, Smith did a very thorough job of killing him, so we were never able to question him about who The Mentor is. We only know that Martel had an accomplice because of what Lydia Chase heard during her imprisonment. She called him 'The Mentor' because he seemed to have taught Martel what he knew about breaking women. We're probably looking for someone older than Martel, so that's at least late thirties. Lydia never got a look at him, so that's really all we have to go on."

"Smith's reports say he suspects The Mentor directly assisted Martel in stalking Lydia after she escaped. Can you tell me more about that?"

"I searched Martel's house after he died." Reed's eyes went impossibly darker as his gaze turned inward. "He kept locks of hair. Eight women. He managed to abduct and murder eight women without drawing attention to himself. He lived completely under the radar. No job, no formal education after dropping out of high school at seventeen. He lived off the money he inherited from his parents when they died the next year. He bought the house he lived in with cash from his inheritance. His one other asset – if you can even call it that – was the white GMC van he used to transport the women. We found hair and blood in the vehicle."

"He sounds like a loner. What makes you think The Mentor helped him terrorize Lydia Chase?"

"Martel wasn't educated, but some of the stunts he pulled while stalking Lydia would have required technological expertise. There was also the incident with the sniper, suggesting a high level of weapons training. We found no evidence of books for tech research in his house, and he wasn't formally educated. He didn't have anything more than a four year old laptop. And he didn't own any guns."

I nodded my agreement with his conclusions. "So he had to have help. It makes sense that The Mentor would have been the person to help him, given Martel's social isolation."

"We need to find out how they met," Reed asserted. "I thought we should start by looking into what might have drawn him to Chicago to abduct Lydia. He must have some ties here. Maybe The Mentor is that tie."

"Considering how Martel lived virtually off the map, it's going to be difficult to track his movements in New York, much less Chicago. Where do you suggest we start?"

"We could go to Dusk, the BDSM club where Martel found Lydia Chase. We can get a list of patrons from the owner. If he won't cooperate, we can try for a subpoena."

"I thought places like that kept people's identities secret?" It came out as a question. This was why we had Reed here.

"A lot of clubs require that patrons pay for membership. They have to give their real personal details as well as scene names. Luckily for us, Dusk is one of those clubs with this policy. We'll be able to look into members for potential ties to Martel."

"That's great." It was better than great. It was the best lead we had come up with in weeks. "We should contact the owner immediately."

Reed frowned at his half-empty cup of coffee. "I guess I'll have to chug this, then."

I rolled my eyes at him. "We have more important things to deal with than your caffeine addiction."

"Hey, I didn't come up with my brilliant idea until I had this coffee, so don't make light of the power of caffeine. Besides, there are worse things to be addicted to." He gestured at my own drink. "Tea, for instance. Disgusting. It tastes like dirty leaves." He shuddered.

"Coffee tastes like burnt dirt," I retorted. "But you can keep your addiction if I can keep mine." I gave him a half-smile. It was amazing how the man was capable of making me smile in the midst of what we were investigating. I loved Dex, but he was always so serious. Reed was levelheaded and lighthearted.

I thought of his quiet rage when I told him about the contents of the note that had been sent to me. He had a fierce side, too, when it mattered.

*"Be careful."* I appreciated Reed Miller's physique far too much for my own good. If I started appreciating his personality as well, I would be well and truly screwed. I wouldn't be able to stand near the man without blushing like a teenager with a crush.

And with my pale skin, blushes were far too obvious. My cheeks would look sunburned.

Reed grinned. "I *can keep my addiction?*" He repeated my words. "How magnanimous of you to allow that, Agent Byrd." His dark eyes were mocking, telling me he didn't need my permission to do anything he wanted.

That damn blush flared, and his grin widened. He knew I was just as affected by his arrogance as I was by his beauty.

"We should go." The words were barely more than a mumble as I cut my eyes to the side.

"Whatever you say." He chuckled, as though he found the idea of following my orders amusing. It should have gotten my hackles up, but – to my embarrassment – it just made heat pulse between my legs.

That sexy little smirk still lingered on his lips as we exited the coffee shop. He held the door for me, like a perfect gentleman. But the wicked gleam of the city lights in his dark eyes was decidedly ungentlemanly. I tore my gaze from his with a murmured "thanks" as I stepped past him. My shoulder grazed his chest, and his warmth pulsed over me. I sidestepped quickly.

*"Be careful."*

We had barely taken ten steps away from the coffee shop when Reed grasped my wrist and hooked my arm through his, pulling my body up tight against him. My gasp was somewhere between shocked and indignant. I gave a little jerk away from him about three heartbeats later than I should have, but he held me fast.

"Reed! This is totally inappropriate!" I wished my voice hadn't wavered.

"Quiet." It was a low order. "Someone's following us. Stay close to me."

I had the good sense not to crane my neck around, but I glanced over at the building to my right. The darkened glass that fronted the closed bank served as a dim mirror in the night. I caught a glimpse of a man wearing a Cubs baseball cap low on his forehead walking twenty paces behind us. The way he angled his face let me know he was trying to conceal his identity. But the man was far too tall and too big to go unnoticed.

My pulse quickened as I snapped my eyes forward. Usually, I wouldn't have been so affected, but the contents of the threatening note were fresh in my mind. Reed was ushering me toward the car a bit faster than what would be considered a natural pace.

"Wait," I hissed. "I am not running from this guy."

His hand tightened around my forearm. "I'm getting you out of here."

"Be sensible, Reed." I demanded as quietly as I could manage while still sounding firm. "We need to catch him. Slow down."

"You're getting in the car and driving to the field office. I'll stay behind and-"

"Oh no you won't," I practically seethed, my anger partially directed at him but also directed at myself for my own weakness. *I'm not scared, I'm not scared.* I gathered my resolve. "I'm an agent, just like you. Let me do my job."

To my amazement, he huffed out a little laugh. "You are so much like Sharon." He said it as though it was a compliment. "All right then, we'll catch him."

Keeping a firm grip on my arm, he steered me around the next corner. The alley was narrow and dimly lit, with no foot traffic. As soon as we were out of sight of the main street, he took me by the shoulders and turned my body so that my back pressed against the concrete building behind me. His hands remained on my shoulders, pinning me in place.

"What are you-?"

"Shhh." His lips nearly brushed mine as he shushed me. Only his hold on my shoulders kept me from leaning forward and closing the distance between us. He smelled so damn good. The scent of coffee clung to him. I suddenly realized that the dark drink must be delicious. I wondered what it would taste like on his lips…

"Just wait." His voice was lower, rougher. My gaze lifted from his lips to his eyes. This close, I could discern the rich espresso of his irises around his dilated pupils. I wasn't the only one affected by our nearness.

But I was the only one who had lost all sense of purpose. I barely remembered why Reed had me in this position until the furious, familiar voice broke through my reverie.

"What the fuck?"

I registered my stalker's identity at the same time as Reed launched himself at the man. Reed's large hands fisted in his shirt, slamming him back against the wall.

"Damn it, Dex!" I shouted. "Reed, wait!"

Reed barely stayed his fist in time to stop it from crunching my friend's nose. Dex was an experienced fighter, but he had obviously been thrown off by the sight of Reed's hands on me. The ire in his glowing blue eyes when he turned them on me told me how intensely it had affected him.

But my anger matched his, and I met his glare. "What the hell are you doing, Dex?" I demanded. "You're following me now?" The Cubs cap should have given him away. How many times had I seen him wear the frayed thing when we went to a game together?

He ground his perfect teeth. "I'm making sure you're safe. You're welcome."

I threw up my hands, exasperated. They had to stop being so protective. It was unnerving. It made the threat real. "What is wrong with you guys? I get one little note and you all freak out over it. It's not a big deal."

"Yes, it is," Dex and Reed snapped at the same time. Dex practically snarled at him, as though he couldn't believe Reed had dared to think about my safety in the same way he did.

They might think they were alpha males, but they were acting like children.

"This is completely ridiculous! We have a serial rapist to catch, and you're wasting your time watching me. No!" I cut them off before their deep voices could start telling me how much danger I was in and how I needed to be protected. "We're focusing on The Mentor from now on. Until the biometric results on the note come back from the lab, there's nothing more we can do about that. I'm a competent agent. I'm grateful for the two of you watching my back, really I am. But there might be a woman suffering right now, and wasting time chasing a ghost that might not exist keeps us from getting to her."

Dex's jaw clenched, and Reed's gaze turned inward.

"Let go of Dex," I ordered Reed.

He blinked, as though he hadn't even realized he was still holding my friend against the wall. His fists unfurled, and Dex helped him step away by giving him a hard shove in the center of his chest.

"Dex, stop being an ass to Reed." Blue eyes blazed as they turned on me, but I lifted my chin and held his hard gaze. After a long moment, he gave a short nod and looked away. I heaved a sigh. God, dealing with these guys was exhausting. I couldn't afford to waste any more energy on them. I needed all my strength to hold myself together in order to maintain the illusion of bravery.

Not looking at either of them, I stalked past the men and back into the swell of people trafficking East Jackson Boulevard. To my surprise, I heard Reed's chuckle behind me. It was followed quickly by Dex's low growl. I glanced back to find them both falling in step behind me. Their paces were casual enough, but I didn't miss the way their eyes surveyed the people around us, searching for my invisible stalker.

I rolled my eyes and focused forward. Anger and appreciation swirled within me. But I forgot both when the Chicago wind whipped up behind me, surrounding me in Reed's scent. I remembered his nearness as he held me against the wall. My shiver wasn't a result of the cool breeze.

# Chapter 4

Stepping into Dusk was a shock to my senses. I had insisted that we speak to the owner as soon as possible, but now I was beginning to regret that. Coming in on a Friday night meant the party was in full swing, and I wasn't prepared for what was going on inside the BDSM club.

The sound of lustful moans and the smell of sex hit me first. It set off my own arousal almost immediately. My clit began to throb as I became acutely aware of how long it had been since I had last been intimate with a man. Thirteen months. Over a year had passed since my breakup with George. It had seemed like nothing, but then I stepped into this kinky haven, and my body became very insistent in reminding me just how deprived I was.

Reed's presence at my side did nothing to help me. His expression was almost one of boredom, a blasé blank that said he had seen it all before and then some. The only time the lines of his face transformed was when his eyes fell on my gaping mouth, and then his own lips ticked up in amusement.

I snapped my teeth closed and tore my eyes from his, but the sights that awaited me only made everything that much worse. The bar where we were waiting for the owner, Josh Dover, was innocuous enough, but it was a burgundy-painted island in the center of the club, separating the dance floor from the dungeon. The scenes unfolding before my eyes made my sex clench.

But woven through my arousal was fear. This was where Lydia Chase had been abducted and taken into a nightmare. Images of her scars and her haunted eyes flashed through my mind. How could I be turned on by what I was seeing? Knowing what she had suffered under the lash made me flinch at the sound of whips striking flesh, even as the resultant moans made my nipples peak against the inside of my bra.

"You all right?" Reed's deep voice and his sudden heat at my side pulled me back to him. When had he gotten so close? And why did the pulsing of my clit ratchet up a notch in response to his nearness?

Unease at my arousal made me edge away, even as the throbbing between my thighs urged me to move into him. The man was magnetic, and my attraction to him was impossibly magnified in this place. His casual bearing plainly declared that this was his domain, and he seemed to have somehow grown larger. I felt small beside him, delicate. And all too breakable. My body enjoyed the sensation, even as my mind instinctively feared weakness. Reed rendered me a study in contradictions, and it was messing with my head.

"Katie?" His expression turned more serious as he prompted my answer. No, not prompted. Demanded.

I did my best to school my features to nonchalance, but my voice came out fainter than I would have liked. "I'm fine."

His brows drew down. "Katie." This time, my name was a sharp warning. "What have I told you about lying to me?"

"What can I do for you?" I blew out a sigh of relief when Josh Dover cut into the tension between us. I turned my attention to the owner of Dusk. He wasn't quite as tall as Reed, but he was broader, harder. The harsh line of his jaw was a bit mean, and his light brown eyes regarded my partner and me with annoyance.

"Mr. Dover." I adopted my official Agent voice and flashed him my Federal credentials. "I'm Agent Byrd, and this is Agent Miller. We have some questions about Lydia Chase."

Dover shook his head. It was a sharp gesture, but his expression turned weary. "I've told you everything I know. Or everything I don't know," he said on a frustrated growl. "How many times do I have to tell you cops that I had nothing to do with her abduction?"

"We're not cops," Reed corrected him calmly. "We're FBI. And we're going to need a list of your patrons. The real list, not scene names."

Dover's jaw firmed. "I won't betray the privacy of my customers. You should know that, Agent Miller." He eyed my partner significantly. The men obviously weren't strangers. It seemed Reed had spent some time in Chicago before joining the FBI.

An image of Reed dressed in the same tight leathers as Dover – and wearing nothing else – bloomed in my mind. It was far too enticing. I wondered if his abs would be just as ripped as Dover's. How would his muscles ripple under his tanned skin when he wielded a whip?

I shook it off before I started drooling, feeling more than a little guilty that I was fantasizing about my partner while I should be tracking down a sadistic killer.

"We will get a subpoena if we have to," I informed Dover.

He turned a dark glare on me, and Reed smoothly moved into my personal space, positioning his body so that it was angled slightly in front of mine. I couldn't help but feel that he was staking a claim over me.

*He's your partner. He's just backing you up,* I reminded myself before I could cook up another lurid and completely inappropriate fantasy.

"Listen, Josh. I don't want it to come to that," Reed addressed the owner with more familiarity. "I swear the identities of your customers will be kept confidential. This is about protecting the people who come here, not outing them."

Dover's glare turned to Reed, but my partner met him with an implacable black stare. After a moment, the owner of Dusk gave a single, nearly imperceptible nod. "I'm trusting you with this, Reed. Don't make me regret it."

"You won't," Reed assured him.

The exchange confirmed my suspicions; the two men did know each other. Reed had visited this BDSM club before. Another vision of him holding a coiled whip, his powerful muscles bulging, flashed across my mind. I told myself my inappropriate thoughts were fueled by the pervasive sights and sounds of sex around me. I told myself they were sick and wrong. But my body couldn't be convinced of that.

Dover left us so he could retrieve the information we had requested, and Reed's attention turned to me. When his eyes met mine, his lips tugged up in a knowing smirk. I felt trapped by that black stare, bound by it. I couldn't have looked away even if I wanted to. I swallowed back the erotic whimper that threatened to ease up my throat. Reed's lips twisted up further. His smile was almost cruel. It made my sex flutter.

"Here." Dover's clipped voice penetrated whatever it was that was passing between us. I blinked and looked away. How long had I been staring up at Reed? It seemed like an all-too-brief eternity.

Blushing furiously, I focused my attention on Dover. He studied me carefully, his eyes flicking from my reddened cheeks to my eyes and back again. I reached out and practically snatched the flash drive from his outstretched hand.

"Thank you, sir." I wasn't sure why I was being so formally polite, but the words seemed to roll off my tongue of their own volition. To my surprise, Dover flashed a smile, his first genuinely warm expression of the evening.

"You're welcome." His eyes turned to Reed. "Let me know if I can do anything else to help."

My brow furrowed. Dover was suddenly very accommodating. I wondered what had changed to make him soften toward us.

"We'll be in touch," Reed told him, his own stance suddenly much more relaxed than it had been since we entered the club. He touched his fingers to my elbow, applying gentle pressure to turn me toward the door. I followed his direction without question. It occurred to me that I should express some sort of indignation at his treatment, but it just wasn't there.

However, the heat he awoke deep within me even with that lightest touch was entirely unprofessional, so I made myself step away from him as I began to walk out of the club. I kept careful distance between us, even once we stepped out into the night. The nearly stifling sexual atmosphere dissipated, but Reed's allure didn't fade.

I caught sight of my black sedan, and annoyance helped pierce my consternation.

"Damn it," I mumbled under my breath in response to the small slip of paper tucked under my windshield wiper. There was no reason to have gotten a parking ticket in the lot for Dusk. I strode forward and snatched it up, grimacing as I braced myself for the damage. But the words on the paper were so much worse than a fine.

*Now, what are you doing at a BDSM club, Kathy?*
*Does my little pet like pain? We are going to get*
*along so well. Come to me and we can play. Come*
*and find me.*

Nausea hit hard, and I swallowed to keep from retching. My skin crawled at the sensation of his eyes on me. He was watching me. I backed away from the car, as though his toxic presence lingered there. I hit something solid, and I whirled to face the threat.

Reed caught my upper arms, preventing me from lashing out. His brows were drawn, his eyes deep pools of concern.

"What is it, Katie?"

*I'm Katie. Not Kathy.* I took a deep breath, clinging to that distinction in order to distance myself from the threat. It wasn't meant for me. The sick fucker who had written the note didn't know me.

Reed released one of my arms to pluck the paper from my fingers, but one hand rose to rest on my shoulder, steadying me. I watched in silence as his eyes darted back and forth, processing the sickening words.

Mere seconds passed before he was crowding me, his large body almost folding over mine as he ushered me to the passenger side of the car. I silently allowed him to guide me into my seat. If I opened my mouth, I would vomit.

*I'm not Kathy. I'm not Kathy.* The mantra did little to soothe me. My denial slipped away from me like a dream upon first awakening.

*"Kathy can be short for Katherine. Don't pretend like you don't know it's for you."* Dex's words rang through my mind with cruel clarity.

Before I could process what was happening, Reed was in the driver's seat, and we were pealing out of the parking lot. Something pressed insistently at the edges of my panic.

"Wait," I rasped. "Go back. We have to go back."

Reed shot me a look that told me I was teetering on the edge of sanity. "No. I'm getting you out of here. He might still be nearby."

"I know! That's why we have to go back," I insisted. "We can't catch him if we're running away."

"I'm calling this in. Dex can case the area. I'm not letting you anywhere near that club."

"Don't be ridiculous, Reed! I'm fine. Turn around."

"You are not fine," he informed me. "And I'm not putting you at risk. He could have a gun."

I had to make him see reason. Even if the cold truth did cut me to the core. "He doesn't want to kill me," I said quietly. "He might still be back there. I don't want to run." The last was a lie.

My heart hammered in my chest, the primal chemicals in my system urging me to flight.

"Too damn bad." Reed dismissed me. He already had his Bluetooth headset hooked into his ear. I zoned out as he put in the call to get the guys out to Dusk. It was much easier to give in, to let go, than to focus on the source of the fear that spread through me like poison.

I retreated into myself, putting up mental walls against my panic. Frank had taught me how to be strong.

*"No one can make you feel powerless unless you give them your permission."* He had told me that once, when he was training me to fight. Even though he was older, he was much bigger than me, and very fit. I had been intimidated, but he encouraged me to stand up to him, to meet his attack and hold my own. That training had saved my ass dozens of times. If I shut down my instinctive fear, if I believed in my abilities, I could be my strongest self.

"What are you doing?" Reed demanded.

"What do you mean?"

"You're burying it. You have to deal with this, Katie. Ignoring it won't solve anything."

*How does he know?* Frank had always told me I was an open book. It seemed Reed could read me just as easily.

"I'm just being practical about it," I countered. I was relieved when my voice came out cool and controlled. "Freaking out over a piece of paper isn't going to solve anything. We'll take it to the lab and get it analyzed, just like the other note. There's nothing more we can do about it now. Especially since we're running away."

"We're not running away. We're just not being stupid. Staying out in the open there would have been a mistake, and you know it. So cut this bullshit bravado and start taking this seriously."

I pursed my lips and shoved my walls up higher. Reed was trying to make me acknowledge my fear, but I couldn't handle that. Fear made me weak, and I couldn't abide weakness. Frank would be disappointed in me if I wasn't brave.

"You don't have to be fearless to be a strong person." Reed's voice was suddenly lower, more soothing.

Those few words threatened to make me come undone. Reed was giving me permission to feel, to let go. Anguish curled up my throat, and it took all my determination to stop my sob. I couldn't give over to my fear. I couldn't make myself vulnerable to it. Steeling myself, I choked down my raging emotions.

"I've seen worse shit than this, Reed. You're new, so you don't get it yet. There are terrible people in the world who do terrible things. Words scrawled on little scraps of paper are nothing compared to what I've seen bad men do."

"Just because you've dealt with horrific things doesn't mean that it's not okay to be afraid. This is a personal threat, Katie, not just another case."

"*Just another case?*" I repeated shrilly. "No case I've worked is 'just another case.' The women I fight for have been horribly abused. I remember each and every one of them. I remember everything that was done to them."

"And now you're scared the same thing will happen to you." Reed met my tirade with the calm truth.

"Just shut up and take me home." It was childish, but I couldn't listen to any more. He was going to break me down, and I wasn't ready to face my emotions. Especially not in front of someone from the Bureau. I was Agent Katherine Byrd, and I didn't cower away from dangerous men. They cowered away from me.

Reed's jaw firmed and remained mercifully closed, but his dark expression told me he was pissed. The beginnings of guilt stirred within me, but I quickly quashed it. I couldn't handle anything more than holding my fear at bay. The only words he spoke were to ask me my address, and then silence stretched between us.

Reed found a parking spot near my apartment block. Before I could finish unbuckling my seatbelt, he was at my door, opening it for me. He took my hand without asking and pulled me to my feet. He was acting too fast for me to process anything but his touch. It wasn't until he began guiding me toward my building that I pieced it together. He was protecting me.

"You don't have to walk me in," I told him. "Whoever left the note can't have followed us. We would have noticed. I'm not-"

Before I could explain to him that I wasn't incompetent, he cut me off with a sharp glare. That was all it took for my mouth to snap closed. Damn, but the man was intimidating when he got like this. I was suddenly glad to have him at my back.

My eyes slid away from his. "Thanks."

"Good." He gave a short nod of approval at my acceptance rather than taking my gratitude with a typical "you're welcome." The gesture smacked of arrogance, but it didn't really bother me. I was used to being on the receiving end of that attitude from Dex. The familiarity was comforting.

"This is me." I fished my keys out of my pocket when we arrived at my door. "Thanks for walking me in."

Again, Reed moved right past the courtesy I offered as though it was a foregone conclusion. "Now that you're being sensible, we can talk about our next steps."

*Our next steps?* "I already told you; I'll take the note to the lab in the morning."

"No. I'll take it now." He didn't ask. He informed. "And tomorrow we're going to look into possible suspects. Before you say anything, you and I will keep our focus on The Mentor. But someone needs to look into this, starting with questioning the men you've put away. Who can help us with that? Dex?"

God, the man was pushy. But I had to admit he was right. I couldn't focus on The Mentor case if I was constantly looking over my shoulder for a stalker.

"Colton Hughes," I sighed the name, resigned. "He's captain of the Chicago PD Special Victims Unit. We've worked together in the past to put away the criminals I've hunted. He's a friend. I'm sure he'll help us look up the status of the prisoners. I don't want Dex on this. We can't afford to distract him, either. He has his own work to do."

*And if I give my friend free reign to track the man down, we'll end up with a dead stalker on our hands.* I didn't want Dex to get in trouble with the Bureau on my account. Because if he found the man who was threatening me, there was no way the perp would get out alive. Colton was fond of me, but he was a bit more level headed than Dex. He was my best option.

"All right," Reed said. "We'll go see Hughes in the morning. And I'm getting the guys at the lab to put a rush on analyzing the notes." His black eyes softened to deepest brown as they focused on me again. He shifted from commanding to comforting in the space of a second. "We'll catch this creep, Katie. You won't have to be scared anymore."

I hauled my walls all the way back up. "I'm not scared."

His expression hardened. "I won't push you tonight, but we're going to have another discussion about lying tomorrow."

I licked my lips nervously. Reed's eyes turned jet black again as they watched my darting tongue.

"Okay," I heard myself agree. "I'll see you tomorrow."

With that, I retreated into my apartment. It was a relief to put the door between myself and my imposing new partner. Exhaustion washed over me, and I leaned back against the wood. So much had happened in the last few hours, and I was overwhelmed by the emotional rollercoaster. I had gone from terror at the first note, to embarrassment in front of Frank, to prying two alpha males away from one another, to arousal at Dusk, and back to terror with the discovery of the second note.

Before I realized it, I slid down to the floor. The door was at my back, and my knees pressed to my chest.

A sound that more closely resembled a scratchy groan than a meow pulled me back to reality. I gave my old ginger tabby a wan smile and scratched him behind the ears.

"Hey, Gizzy."

Gizmo always knew when I needed a furry shoulder to cry on. All too often, animals were far kinder to me than humans. The scumbags I hunted every day were proof of the horrors man was capable of inflicting on others.

"I should have been a vet," I told my cat. It was something I never admitted aloud, but Gizmo would keep my secret. I had always wanted to work with animals, but Frank convinced me that the work I could do for the FBI was more important. And while I did get a sense of satisfaction out of putting heinous criminals behind bars, my job was more upsetting than I would ever say to Frank, or even Dex.

*"No one can make you feel powerless unless you give them your permission."* Frank was right. I wasn't weak. He had helped me fully realize my own power, and I was grateful to him for that. I had felt so helpless after my father's death, but Frank had stepped in and shown me how to be strong.

I could handle pain, mental and physical. My second father had taught me how.

*Does my little pet like pain? We are going to get along so well.* The sickening words seared across my brain. I ran to the bathroom and vomited.

# Chapter 5

Colton ran a hand through his shaggy blond hair, and his chiseled jaw clenched with anger. Disgust twisted his lips and accentuated the fine lines around his dark chocolate eyes.

"Don't be like that, Colton," I ordered before he could start acting like Dex and Reed. "I'm fine. I just need help catching this guy so I can focus on my work."

The older man fixed me with a stern glare, and I resisted the urge to shuffle towards Reed for backup. "Tell me what the notes said. Word for word."

I swallowed against the lump in my throat. It blocked the horrifying words. Instead of complying, I managed to circumvent his demand. I gestured at the folder I had placed in front of him. "You have copies of the notes right there."

His brows rose. "I know what they say. But if you're fine, why can't you read them out to me?"

"Katie is having trouble with lying lately," Reed remarked.

Colton's attention focused on him for the first time, and the captain's eyes narrowed as he sized up my partner. Some form of silent communication passed between the two men, and after a moment, Colton inclined his head slightly.

This was getting old fast. Didn't they realize I could handle myself? I clearly wasn't doing a good job of convincing them. I ground my teeth. "Are you going to help me or not?"

Colton's eyes returned to mine, and I suddenly felt pinned in place by his intense gaze. "Both the notes say 'Come and find me.' He obviously wants you to try to track him down on your own. That means he has some sort of trap planned. So yes, I will help you, because you're not going anywhere near this."

"Fine." Snappishness masked my secret relief. "I'll stay away from it, because I have a more important case to deal with. I don't need a distraction."

His gaze turned impossibly harder. "This is more than just a distraction. It's a serious threat. I'm going to look into the men you've locked up. Whoever this is has a personal vendetta. I don't know how one of them would get these notes to you, but maybe he has an accomplice on the outside."

"Is there anyone you know personally who might be behind this?" Reed asked me. "An ex, maybe?"

I immediately shook my head. "George wouldn't do this. He's a good guy."

*He might have been a great guy, if he hadn't broken it off so suddenly.* I really should have taken that up with Frank, but I didn't have the guts to accuse him of running off my boyfriend. I couldn't bring myself to rail at him for looking out for me. I wasn't going to spurn the only father I had left.

"I'll look into him," Colton told Reed.

I fought the urge to stamp my foot like an ignored child seeking attention. "I'm telling you, George wouldn't do something like this. We only went out for a few months, and he was the one who left. And that was over a year ago. He has no reason to want to hurt me."

"Then I'll wait until I see what turns up with the inmates," Colton allowed. "But I'm going to question him if nothing comes from that."

"Damn it, Colton, I came to you because I thought you would be reasonable about this. Why aren't you listening to me?"

"I'm being perfectly reasonable," he told me coolly. "And I am listening to you. I said I would only question George if it came to that. Look me in the eye and tell me we wouldn't go to the ex-boyfriend first if this case was about some other woman."

*Damn it.* I shifted my weight and cut my eyes away from his. Of course we would look at the ex first in a case like this.

"That's what I thought," he said with grim satisfaction. His voice turned gentler a moment later. "I'll take care of this, Katie. And I'll keep you informed every step of the way."

I blew out a long breath, some of my irritation leaving me. "Thanks, Colton. I appreciate it."

"No problem." His attention turned to Reed. "You look out for her until we catch this fucker."

"I will," Reed promised.

Could they be any more high-handed? I pushed back my irritation. I would deal with my partner later. We needed to have a conversation about gender equality.

"Call me if you find anything."

Colton nodded in response to my request, and I turned to leave. I couldn't wait to get out of his office and away from the two domineering men. Reed had proven to be infuriating at times, but having both of them gang up on me was galling. It was time I talked to my partner about respecting his peers.

Reed flanked me like a bodyguard, even though we were in the police station. I was perfectly safe here. I waited until we were in the privacy of my car to lay into him. I couldn't allow him to keep acting like this. Not if I was going to maintain the respect of the guys at the office. Not if I was going to keep up the charade that nothing about my job ever got to me.

"Listen, Miller." His surname was cold on my tongue. "I don't know what you think you're playing at, but your behavior is unacceptable. You're new to the Bureau, so maybe you don't get it yet. You can't treat me like this. I might only be a couple years older than you, but that means I have two years of experience on you. If anything, you should defer to me, not the other way around. I want to work with you as a partner, but that's not going to work if you don't see me as an equal."

To my surprise, he gave me a wry smile. "You are so much like Sharon," he told me again. He said it with fondness. "She doesn't like being protected, either. But she's also learned not to be stupid enough to take things on by herself. Would you have gone to Colton for help if I hadn't asked you to?"

I huffed out a breath and sidestepped the question. "You didn't exactly *ask*. You can't be so controlling. That's not what partnership is about."

His light expression turned more serious. "I am controlling, when I need to be. I'm an FBI agent, but I'm also a Dom. I'm going to be demanding when it comes to protecting you. That's my job as your partner, and that's who I am as a man."

A few heartbeats of silence passed as his black eyes bored into mine, impressing upon me the significance of his words. This was who Reed Miller was, and I could choose to either accept that or not. The forbidding glint in his eyes let me know that not accepting wasn't in my best interest.

The flush that crept up my neck to flood my cheeks let me know that my body very much wanted to accept him. That dark stare did something to me. It awoke an answering darkness deep within me, something that was both fiercely hungry and softly pliant at the same time. I wanted, but I would wait. Because that was what he desired. Reed's will washed over me, and I didn't even try to fight it. Fighting was exhausting, especially when what he was offering was so alluring; protection, comfort.

"Now, I believe we were going to discuss your lying." He kept me locked in his gaze. "It's okay to be afraid, Katie. It's natural. Being afraid doesn't mean you're not brave. Your bravery is defined by how you face your fear. And facing it alone isn't brave; it's foolish. It's dangerous."

*"You don't have to be fearless to be a strong person."* Reed's words from the day before reminded me that I didn't have to do this on my own.

I dropped my eyes, suddenly ashamed of my pigheaded denial of the truth that everyone could see: I was facing some scary shit. Accepting that was the first step to conquering it.

"Look at me, Katie." My eyes snapped to Reed's instantly in response to his stern order. "You're going to be honest with me from now on. And you're going to be honest with yourself. Colton's right. Whoever is sending these notes wants you to seek him out on your own. Don't isolate yourself in your own fear. Because that's what will happen if you deny it. True strength is found in accepting every part of yourself, even the parts you're not so proud of."

Something flashed in his eyes at the last, an inner pain that I was able to glimpse in his moment of raw honesty. Reed had obviously wrestled his own demons in the past.

His words were a revelation. They were so different from how I viewed inner strength. In my efforts to make Frank proud, I had buried every trace of vulnerability for the last nine years. Now that I was faced with the threat of this sick stalker, I realized that my strength was a fragile thing. It was the illusion of strength, not the true power I saw in Reed.

His chin lifted, and I suddenly felt much smaller under the weight of his imperious stare. "You're not going to lie anymore, Katie. Tell me you'll always be honest with me."

"I won't lie to you, Reed," I promised softly.

"Good." His approval was a deep rumble. My heart skipped a beat when he reached for me. My body remained frozen in place as his thumb gently brushed the single tear that had rolled down my cheek.

*Shit.* I pulled back and swiped at the wetness on my face. I never cried. I couldn't. Frank had taught me how to bottle up my tears, how to be brave. But Reed was tempting me to allow my vulnerability to bleed out into the open.

*Maybe Frank was wrong. Maybe burying my emotions makes me even more vulnerable when shit really hits the fan. I don't know how to handle them.*

I shook the thought away almost angrily and turned the key in the ignition with more force than was necessary. I didn't look at

Reed as I drove back to the field office, but I could feel his disapproval pulsing over me. Mercifully, he didn't push me. He seemed to sense that I had taken as much as I could for the time being. I was grateful for his perceptiveness, even if I was deeply troubled by our conversation about personal honesty. Being honest with him was one thing; not lying to myself was another entirely.

By the time I pulled into the parking garage, I had managed to get a handle on my emotions. Frank was waiting upstairs, and I wasn't going to let him see how shaken up I was.

Luckily, it didn't come to that. When I stepped out of the elevator, I found that Frank was in his office with the blinds closed, a sure sign he didn't want to be bothered. I thought about knocking on his door anyway to tell him I had enlisted Colton's help in investigating the notes. He would want to know about that.

Dex saved me from making the decision. His large body appeared in front of me, as though he had been waiting for me to arrive.

"Where have you been?" He demanded. His eyes cut to Reed where he stood at my side.

My brows rose. "Hello to you, too."

My friend grimaced. "I've done some digging on Martel. I need to talk to you."

"Okay. Let's talk." I began to walk past him towards my desk.

His hand closed around my elbow, stopping me short. I glanced up at him in surprise. It wasn't like Dex to put his hands on me.

"You didn't answer my question. I got a call to come out to Dusk last night because you've received another threat, and you didn't even call me to tell me about it personally. Where have you been?"

"I went to see Colton. He's going to help look into the status of the prisoners I've put away to see if any of them might be involved with the notes I've received. I'm dealing with it."

Rather than allaying his anger, my admission of having involved someone else in the matter further enraged him. "You should have come to me." The words were harsh, almost accusatory. I knew him well enough to recognize that his ferocity masked hurt.

"I didn't want to worry you," I told him. "You have more important things to focus on, and so do I. Colton is helping us out so that we can focus on our jobs. I won't let this creep distract me from catching The Mentor. And on that note, I would appreciate hearing this new intel on Martel."

I pulled away from him, firmly extricating my elbow from his grip. His jaw ticked at my taking charge, but he followed behind me as I resumed my progress towards my desk. I could almost feel his irritation increase when Reed remained by my side. I felt a little guilty for the slight to Dex, but I wasn't going to go out of my way to make him happy when he was acting like an imperious ass.

By the time Dex pulled a chair up across from mine – straddling it, per usual – and Reed settled down beside me, my friend had schooled his expression to something more neutral.

"I think Martel murdered his adoptive parents," he said without preamble.

"Why?" I wasn't shocked by the information – I knew the horrors Martel had been capable of – but I was interested in how Dex had come to that conclusion.

"Our records show that Martel dropped out of high school at seventeen, and that he inherited everything from his parents when they died six weeks later."

I nodded. "It was a car accident. They lost control and drove into the Jamesville Reservoir."

"I had forensics go back over the case. The level of decomposition of the bodies when they were found doesn't match up with their supposed time of death. Martel said his parents had driven to Syracuse and not returned for two weeks, when they were supposed to have been gone for one.  Police began a search and recovered their bodies from the water six days after Martel filed the report.  It was dismissed as an accident, but decomp suggests their bodies were in the water for much longer than the few weeks that Martel claimed."

"So you think he staged the accident."

Dex nodded.  "He filed the report the day after his eighteenth birthday.  I think he killed them around the time he dropped out of Lincoln High School, and he waited to report them missing until he was legally an adult.  That way he could cleanly inherit everything they had and start living his life under the radar."

"That's great Dex.  I mean, that's good work.  So Martel killed his only family.  Where does The Mentor come into this?  Who would Martel trust enough to form that kind of bond?"  As sick as it was, it did take some level of emotional connection to entrust one person with his secret crimes, to share in his brutality with a kindred spirit.

*My job is so fucked up.*  I hated that I even had to think things like this.

"Well, like you said, Katie, he had no other family," Reed interjected.  "And we don't know his bio parents.  He was anonymously dropped at a hospital, so it's unlikely that he was able to track them down, either."

I didn't get a chance to ponder how this new intel on Martel's parents fit into the puzzle.  My thoughts were obliterated by the sound of Frank's voice booming through the office.

"Byrd.  My office.  Now."

*Oh.  Shit.*  That tone usually made even the toughest agents look like they wanted to run in the opposite direction.  Frank had never used it on me before.  What had I done wrong?

"Do you want me to go with you?" Reed asked kindly.

"I'll go," Dex almost barked at him.

"Neither of you are coming." I couldn't deal with them. Not when I had my own fear to wrestle down. Besides, I had a feeling Frank would be even more furious if I brought one of them with me. The last thing I needed was for another alpha to challenge my dad when he was mad at me. Neither of them would win going head-to-head with Frank, no matter how good their intentions.

I wasn't sure how I had gotten there, but suddenly I found myself at the threshold of Frank's office. I seemed to have floated there, pulled to him by the power of his will. The door was ajar, and his anger slammed into me as soon as I crossed into his office.

"Close the door." The order was low, dangerous. I obeyed immediately. My fingers trembled as I pressed them against the wood. The click of the latch sliding home seemed to crack behind me like the report of a rifle.

It took all my determination to look Frank in the eye. His stony expression made me glance away instantly, and my eyes found a spot on the floor just beside the toes of my shiny black flats. He didn't ask me to sit down, so I stood there, waiting to be reprimanded for whatever transgression I had committed.

"Can you explain to me why I just received a call from Colton Hughes regarding your stalker." It wasn't a question.

"I…" The word was a squeak. I swallowed and tried again. "I didn't want to distract anyone at the Bureau with it, so I went to him for help."

"So you just thought you could go to the CPD with FBI business and I wouldn't find out about it?"

"No!" Shit. I hadn't thought about it like that. "I asked him to help me with a personal problem, not a Federal investigation. I wouldn't go behind your back on a case."

"That's exactly what you did. I told you to come to me about this, Katie. You deliberately disobeyed me."

"I didn't." Tears threatened, but I pushed them back. I couldn't cry in front of Frank. "I didn't think-"

"No. You didn't think. That's why we're having this conversation."

He sighed, and the wheels of his office chair squealed as he pushed back from his desk. His arms were around me seconds later, pulling me into his embrace. I couldn't resist the comfort it offered. I returned the hug fiercely. It wasn't often that Frank held me like this. He hadn't since shortly after my father died. But I needed it now almost as badly as I had then.

With one final squeeze, he pulled back from me, but he left his hands resting on my shoulders. I was grateful that he didn't completely break contact. I needed his strength, his support. How could I have allowed myself to disappoint him when he only ever had my best interests in mind?

"I'm sorry."

He gave me a small smile, and just like that, all of my anguish was lifted. "I know you are. Just don't do anything like that again. You need to let me take care of this, Katie. I don't trust your safety to anyone else. Do you understand?"

Emotion welled up in me. This was the Frank I loved. So serious but so strong. He would see me through anything.

"Yes. Thanks, Frank."

"You're welcome. Now, Colton gave me some disturbing news. Apparently Claude Parnell managed to weasel his way out of jail."

My heart skipped a beat. "What?" The serial rapist I had arrested only weeks earlier was free? "How?"

"Something about evidence being lost. They couldn't hold him without it." He speared me with a significant stare. "Parnell is most likely the one behind the threats. You remember how he acted toward you when you brought him in."

Oh, I remembered. His murky eyes had devoured me, and his lewd comments had been so sick that I almost walked out of interrogation. Frank himself had finally stepped in to shut him up.

"So we have no idea where Parnell is now?" I asked as steadily as I could manage.

Frank's mouth twisted down in disgust. "No. But we're looking for him. I asked Colton to put some men on it. We'll find him. I'll take care of you, Katie."

I nodded, knowing my voice would break if I tried to speak. Frank was so good to me. He was tough as a rock, but he loved me. Looking up into his hard eyes, I could see his determination to protect me. If he caught Parnell, the man would never see the light of day again. The knowledge filled me with grim satisfaction.

# Chapter 6

Desire rolled through me, the heat of it contrasting sharply with the cool air that caressed my naked flesh. My skin pebbled, and I shivered from something more than the cold. My core throbbed, aroused to the point of sweet pain. It tried to touch myself to ease the ache, but something bit into my wrists, holding my arms firmly over my head. My entire body jerked with instinctive fear, and I realized that rope bound my ankles as well. I was tied to my bed, my arms and legs stretched wide, leaving me open and vulnerable.

A low chuckle teased across my neck, and black eyes appeared above mine. Reed's weight settled over me, pressing me down into the mattress. Fear morphed into lust, and I rocked my hips up into him. His cock was hard against my belly, and I craved for him to thrust into me and end my sensual torment.

His grin was sharp-edged as he remained motionless, denying me. The fire within me flared hotter. I enjoyed his power over me, reveling in finally allowing myself to let go, I could be vulnerable with Reed. The satisfaction I found in that was more than just emotional. It made my body burn for him.

He lowered his lips to my throat, pressing hot kisses against my sensitized skin, tracing the line of my collarbone with his tongue. I craved to hold him, to pull him closer. My hands tugged uselessly against the restraints, and the feel of the rough rope tightening around my wrists made me moan as I was reminded of my own powerlessness at his hands.

He laughed again, but this time the sound was colder somehow. It sent a chill racing through the heat that pulsed at my core.

"Reed…" Uncertainty made his name waver as it left my lips.

Suddenly, his teeth closed around my hardened nipple. It was a harsh, cruel bite, and it sent a shock of true pain crashing through my arousal. I cried out, but he didn't relent. His fingernails dug into my other nipple.

"Reed! You're hurting me. Stop!"

His black eyes snapped up to mine. No, not black. Muddy green.

*Martel.* His teeth were red with my blood when he grinned down at me. I screamed and twisted against my bonds as terror engulfed me. His cock twitched against my thigh.

"Does my little pet like pain? We are going to get along so well." His voice oozed over me like toxic slime.

I tried to scream again, but no sound came out. I was restrained, silenced, completely powerless. All of my training counted for nothing. I had willingly allowed him to trap me. I had enjoyed my bonds only moments before. This was sick, wrong. How could I have ever found lust in this vulnerability?

Martel's face wavered above me, rippling as though it was a reflection in water. When it smoothed again, Dex's electric blue eyes stared down at me. His expression was drawn into the same cruel leer, his reddened teeth bared in twisted pleasure.

My stomach churned. "No."

*Not Dex. Not Dex.*

Pain and horror wracked my body as I tore my skin with my struggles. Dex threw back his head and laughed. When it lowered again, Colton was grinning down at me.

How could the men who cared for me be capable of such cruelty? How could they relish my pain?

Colton blinked, and then Frank's eyes bored into me.

I shrieked and jolted upright. My body should have collided with his, but there was nothing there. I blinked hard, and my empty bedroom coalesced around me as my eyes adjusted to the darkness. Sweat soaked my hair, and my body shook uncontrollably. I raised my wrists before my eyes, studying them for rope abrasions. Nothing. My skin was smooth and whole.

*A dream. It was just a dream.*

The realization did little to quell the terror that still raged within me. I felt dirty, violated. And by men I loved.

All this talk of Doms and BDSM and allowing myself to be vulnerable to my emotions was messing with my head. My lust for Reed and the dark sensuality he exuded was poison to my psyche. The secret desires he stirred within me would ruin me if I acted on them. I had seen what had been done to Lydia Chase. That was what happened if a woman gave up sexual power to a man. That was what came of enjoying pain with sex.

*"Does my little pet like pain?"*

I shuddered. I couldn't quite shake the feel of cruel hands upon me. The faint light tricking through my blinds let me know dawn was coming. It was far too early to get up – usually I slept in as late as possible – but no way was I going to be able to fall back asleep. I was too frightened of what horrific scenes would play out behind my closed eyelids.

My knees wobbled when I pushed myself to my feet, but I managed a drunken walk to my bathroom. I cranked up the shower until it was scalding hot and then stepped under the spray. The sound of the pounding water smothered my sobs, and the warm droplets rolling down my cheeks masked my tears. I was glad of that. I couldn't allow myself to acknowledge that I was a blubbering mess.

*I am not weak. I am not weak.*

I repeated the mantra in my head and sucked in deep breaths. They burned as I forced them down my constricted throat, but my sobs quieted.

By the time my fingertips became wrinkled, I had stopped my shameful tears. Martel was dead. He couldn't hurt me. I wasn't afraid of a dream.

The lie was comforting, the practice familiar. If I just told myself I wasn't scared, the fear would go away. Frank had taught me that. He had also taught me that throwing myself into work helped me take my mind off my own emotions. Entering that cool, composed place allowed me to delve into the lives of heinous criminals and it allowed me to detach from my own problems as well.

I opened my laptop and plugged in the flash drive that Josh Dover had given us. Gizmo jumped up onto the couch and settled in beside me, pressing against my thigh with furry, comforting warmth. I had been researching the patrons of Dusk for nearly two hours when my buzzer shattered my almost trance-like concentration. Usually, I would have cussed up a storm at someone stopping by my apartment at this hour. I wasn't one to throw around colorful swear words casually, but waking me up early was a sure way to bring out my inner grouch.

This time, my grumpiness was for other reasons. Losing myself in work had been a relief, and now my morning visitor was shredding that, pulling me back to reality.

The buzzer sounded again.

"Wait just a fucking second, asshole." My cursing was in full swing, despite the fact that I had been awake for hours. I really wasn't fit for human interaction before eight AM.

"Who is it?" I almost snapped into my receiver.

"Good morning to you, too, sunshine. It's Reed. Let me in."

"You could ask, you know," I informed him testily.

"I know."

A little exasperated noise huffed out of my chest, but I buzzed him up. My toe tapped a staccato beat on the floor while I waited for him to arrive. I practically wrenched the door open with my irritation when I heard the first knock.

"Please, for the love of god, tell me you have coffee." His voice was a low rumble, made rougher than usual by weariness.

His captivating eyes were bloodshot, and his formerly crisp white collared shirt was rumpled.

"What happened to you?"

The ghost of a smile played around his lips. "Aren't you just a peach in the morning?" With that, he stepped forward, forcing me to back up and admit him. I didn't even process the fact that he had entered without my invitation. I just moved aside as I studied him quizzically.

"Did you pull an all-nighter?"

"Yep." He strode into my small, narrow kitchen as though he owned the place. His eyes scanned the countertop, and he frowned. "You really don't have a coffee pot. How do you live like this?" The look he shot me was one of admonition. "You would be more pleasant in the mornings with a little caffeine, you know."

I ignored the jibe. "You should have called me to let me know you were working last night. I would have come into the office with you and helped out."

"I wasn't at the office."

My brows drew together. He didn't strike me as the type to stay out at bars all night when he was working a case. Unless he was with a woman…

"Where were you, then?" My question was a touch more incisive than I would have liked.

"Outside your place." He shrugged, as though that information was of little consequence.

I blinked, taken aback. "You slept in your car? Why?"

His expression told me I was being a bit slow. "I didn't sleep. I was keeping an eye out for your stalker. Now that we know who to look for, I wanted to make sure Parnell was nowhere near your apartment."

A long moment of silence passed as that sank in. I knew Reed wanted to protect me, but I hadn't thought he would go so far as to keep watch over me. I suddenly felt guilty for being so snappish when he first arrived.

"Sorry I don't have any coffee," I said softly, at a loss as to what else to say.

He smiled. "I'm sorry, too. You look like you could use some." He took inventory of me. I was sure my eyes were as red as his, and I probably had ugly dark circles under them. "Rough night?"

"I couldn't sleep," I admitted.

It suddenly struck me that I was wearing my ratty old sweatpants and a thin camisole. And I wasn't wearing a bra. Of course, as soon as I realized that, my nipples hardened. Reed's eyes flicked to my chest, and his nostrils flared before he lifted his gaze back to my face.

I bit my lip and looked away, my cheeks flaming.

"I, um… I think I have eggs in the fridge. Can I make you breakfast?"

"I'd rather have a shower and change, if you don't mind." Reed hefted a small tote bag that I hadn't noticed hanging at his side.

He hadn't even gone home to get dressed?

"You didn't have to do that," I told him. "You didn't have to watch my place. I can look out for myself."

"I know I didn't have to, and I know you can. That doesn't change the fact that I did. Now, can I take a shower here or are we going to my hotel?"

"*We?*"

He nodded. "I'm not leaving you alone until we catch this guy."

I stared at him for a moment, dumbfounded. He stared back, waiting.

"Just give me a sec." I found myself darting into my room. I threw my covers back in a semblance of having made my bed, and I hastily tugged on my work clothes. It was a relief to know that my peaked nipples were concealed by my bra and blouse when I returned to the small living room.

"Okay." I jerked my thumb at my bedroom door, letting him know he could pass. "You can take a shower. Towels are in the linen closet to the right of the sink." An image of him under the hot spray flashed across my mind. Reed Miller was going to be naked. In my shower. With only one thin wall separating us.

He smirked as he took in my pink cheeks. "Thanks."

He brushed past me before I could make my brain function properly again. His scent wafted over me, further impeding my ability to think. Half a minute passed before I realized I was standing frozen in the middle of my living room.

*Idiot.* Reed probably thought the same. His smirk told me as much. I had caught glimpses of desire from him, like when his gaze had riveted on my chest only minutes earlier, but he didn't seem as strongly affected by me as I was by him.

And why would he be? I was nothing special. I wasn't some bombshell or enticing temptress. Hell, I had only had sex with one guy other than George, and that had been one drunken night in college. I had been a twenty-one year old virgin, and I decided I needed to do something about it. The sex had been so lackluster that I hadn't really gotten what all the fuss was about. I only had sex with George four years later because it seemed like the right thing to do. We were adults in a committed relationship. Wasn't that what people did?

But George hadn't ignited passion within me, either. What we shared didn't come close to the steamy scenes in the books I secretly stored on my Kindle. Alpha males; bondage; spankings.

I hadn't dared to pick up my ereader since I came across Lydia Chase's case.

But now… My closely-guarded fantasies were bleeding into my reality when it came to Reed Miller. I spent plenty of time around alpha males, but he was the only out-and-proud Dominant I knew. That knowledge did funny things to my insides.

If I was being honest, it was more than just the knowledge that did it for me. Reed was gorgeous, and a flirt at that. What woman could resist fantasizing about him?

I recalled the Reed in my dream, the way he had incited my lust as he bound me, teasing me. An echo of that heat flared between my legs, even as my mind tangled around the way he had changed into Martel and hurt me.

*Wrong.* No matter what Reed said, no matter how good he was, BDSM was wrong. It would bring me nothing but grief.

*"Does my little pet like pain?"*

"You okay?" I jolted at Reed's voice.

*Crap.* I was still standing where he had left me, frozen in my brooding.

"I'm-" I was about to tell him I was fine, but the lie died in my throat when I turned to him. His black eyes and taut lips forbade my dishonesty. I sighed. "I'm just a little off this morning. I didn't sleep well last night."

His expression softened. "Bad dreams?"

"Yeah." My voice was small, but I told the truth.

"Want to talk about it?"

"No." I was grateful he had given me the option. No way was I going to admit to my kinky dream about him. And I didn't want to tell him how he had turned into Martel. I got the feeling he wouldn't appreciate that. I recalled how angry he had become when he accused me of thinking he was like Martel, that he enjoyed abusing women. No, I definitely wasn't willing to tell him about my messed-up dream.

"Okay," he capitulated easily. "Let's get some coffee, then. I don't know how much longer I can make it without going into withdrawals."

It struck me all over again that he had gone without sleep to watch over me. He looked more refreshed after his shower, but I knew he must be exhausted. I continued to study him anyway, helpless to stop myself. His black hair was slick with water and mussed where he had run the towel over it to dry it. He looked slightly messy. He wasn't wearing his suit jacket, and his black tie was loosened. It was so different from the smoothly cultured look he usually portrayed. This was a wilder, more intimate side of Reed, the real man behind the carefully controlled FBI agent. And yet, he still radiated that same sense of power. If anything, it was more potent, as though the trappings of everyday life kept it leashed.

I was suddenly aware of how close he was. I could feel the heat of his body pulsing towards mine, almost as though it was reaching out for me. I didn't understand why he seemed to be drawn to me, why he was so concerned with protecting me. The man hardly knew me.

"Why?" I breathed, truly baffled as to why he would go to such lengths to keep me safe. "Why are you looking out for me like this?" A cruel conclusion was my first answer. My gaze narrowed. "Do you think I need a babysitter?"

He stepped right into my personal space, and his heat enveloped me. "No. I think you need a Dom." His voice was deep, the statement an absolute. His hand curled around the back of my neck, tenderly caressing at first, then gripping me firmly when I didn't protest. I couldn't even begin to formulate an objection. My skin sparked where he touched me, and when his fingers tightened around my nape, something softened deep within me.

My instinct to fight was utterly absent. My body became strangely light, pliant, and my will bent to his. It was automatic, a natural response to his dominance. The pressure of his fingers against the side of my throat increased, and my head dropped back. Light reflected off his polished ebony eyes as they flashed with satisfaction. My lips parted in invitation, and his descended on mine.

His kiss was deliberate; there was nothing hurried about the way his mouth moved over mine, but his lips firmly demanded that mine shape to his. I sighed into him, and his hand slid up into my hair, slowly curling into a fist, increasing the pull on the copper strands until tingles raced across my scalp in response to the delicious little pain of it. His arm wrapped around me, and his hand found the small of my back, pressing my hips into his.

Even as lust flared, it was the intimidating size of his thick erection that brought me back to my senses. Images from my dream flashed across my mind, and I remembered how desire at his hard cock against me had morphed to terror.

I stiffened beneath him, and my hands came up to press against his chest. The feel of his hard muscles tightening beneath my fingers almost made me melt all over again, but Reed was already pulling away.

My breath came in little pants as I stared up at him, and his eyes clouded over with his own confusion. He took a careful step back.

"I'm sorry," he said, but his voice held no contrition. "That was inappropriate."

I blushed and looked away. "Yes," I agreed. "It was wrong."

His fingers curled under my chin, lifting my face to his. When I met his gaze, I found that his expression was stern. "No. I'll apologize for kissing you because we're coworkers, and that was inappropriate. But it wasn't wrong. I meant what I said, Katie. You need a Dom. You need someone to help you let go and make you see that it's okay to be vulnerable. And you naturally crave that submission."

I shook my head. "Reed, I-"

"Don't deny it," he rode over me smoothly. "You're not allowed to lie, remember?"

My teeth sank into my lower lip. "Yes. I remember."

Reed blinked and stepped away again, releasing me from his touch. I rocked forward slightly as my body protested the loss.

"You need a Dom, and I won't deny that my instincts are to fill that need. You're innocent and submissive and beautiful, and you need a firm hand to make you see sense when it comes to protecting yourself." His eyes darkened. "Do you have any idea how goddamn irresistible you are?"

Unease stirred through my dumbfounded moment of flattery. "Reed, I… I don't want this. I mean," I said quickly before he could warn me against lying, "I'm scared of this. I shouldn't want to be made vulnerable. Not after everything I've seen…" I trailed off, unable to compare Reed to Martel. The two men were nothing alike, but that didn't stop my subconscious from fearing submission. I was afraid to willingly make myself powerless.

Reed's lips thinned, and the lingering lust seeped from his features. "Okay, Katie," he finally allowed. "I can understand that. I won't push you to be something you don't want to be."

I blew out a relieved breath. "Thank you."

He nodded curtly, his expression disapproving despite his capitulation.

"Come on," I said to break the tension. "Let's get breakfast. I might even try coffee. If I load it up with sugar, it might be bearable."

Just like that, Reed's levity returned. He gave a dramatic shudder, but his smile was back. "Blasphemy," he declared. "You drink it black, or you don't drink it at all. I'll teach you to like it."

I nodded my surrender. Oh, I was sure Reed could teach me to like a lot of things.

# Chapter 7

"Take a bite of the iced lemon cake first," Reed instructed from where he sat across from me at Starbucks. I tore off a chunk of yellow cake and obediently popped it between my lips. It was sweet and tangy. "Now drink." Reed pushed the cup of black coffee toward me. I eyed it warily. "Katie." My name was a stern admonishment for hesitating.

I reached forward and plucked up the paper cup. My sip was tentative. I hadn't tried coffee since I was eleven. I had sneaked a swig out of my dad's thermos one day and deemed it disgusting.

This was different. The bitter liquid mingled with the sweetness of the cake on my tongue, morphing it into something rich and boldly flavorful.

"See?" Reed said triumphantly. "The lemon cake works with the citrus notes in this blend. You'll be an addict like the rest of us soon enough."

I laughed. "I don't think anyone I know is as much of an addict as you are. The *citrus notes?* This isn't a wine tasting, Reed."

He grinned at me. "No, it's better. Wine is gross."

"What would you prefer? Irish coffee?" I teased.

"Something like that. But I'm a microbrew man, really."

"Microbrew? Citrus notes in coffee? Oh my god, are you a hipster?"

"I don't know, am I? I like to think I just have discerning tastes. Although I have been considering growing a scraggly beard and wearing baggy striped sweaters…"

I held up a hand. "Don't even joke about that."

"What, you don't think I could pull it off?"

"No. I mean, yes." I fumbled. The man would look gorgeous no matter what he wore.

His grin turned crooked. "So you like the way I look?"

I rolled my eyes to cover how flustered I had become. "You know you're pretty. You don't need me to tell you that to feed your ego."

"Oh, my ego is always hungry." His expression shifted to something wolfish. "I like the way you look, too, Katie." He eyed me with flagrant appreciation.

I didn't understand how he could think that, but the attraction between us was undeniably potent.

*"You're innocent and submissive and beautiful."* I could hardly believe Reed had spoken those words. No one thought I was beautiful. Well, George had said I was pretty. And the criminals I brought in always had something sickeningly appreciative to say about my body. No one else had ever shown any interest.

*No one ever got close enough to show interest.* I supposed Frank's shadow had always loomed large over me. Most men cowered in his presence, so I guessed it wasn't such a surprise that I hadn't had more than one boyfriend since he took me under his wing. Besides, I worked so hard to make him proud that I hadn't really allowed myself time for relationships. And now the first man who truly enflamed me was off-limits.

I tore my eyes from Reed's. "That's enough of that," I mumbled.

His lips turned down at the corners, but he wisely let it drop. He pushed back in his seat, putting more distance between us. When had he leaned into me? I resisted the temptation to angle my body forward to keep him close. We were like magnets, drawn together when we weren't actively resisting. Somehow, Reed wanted me as badly as I wanted him.

*He wants you because you're submissive,* a mean little voice reminded me. He had told me I needed a Dom, and he naturally wanted to fulfil that role. While the idea of Reed dominating my body got me hotter than I would have thought possible before I met him, it still scared me more than a little bit. That fear was convenient. It was all that kept me from jumping his bones. Or begging him to jump mine. I had a feeling I wouldn't be the aggressor in any of our sexual interactions. Reed wouldn't allow it.

His lips took on a regretful twist, and I realized I was staring again.

Fear. Yes, fear was definitely better than lust. I focused on the horrors of my dream to dispel my need for my partner's touch. My face must have betrayed my disgust, because Reed's brow wrinkled with concern.

"You had that look when I came to your apartment this morning. Are you going to tell me what's bothering you?"

I pursed my lips. *Don't lie.*

"No," I said honestly. "I don't want to talk about it. Let's get to the office before Dex sends out a search."

Thankfully, Reed agreed without pressing for more. I was also grateful that Dex wasn't waiting for me when I stepped out of the elevator and into the office. I didn't want him to see me arrive with Reed, especially not when we both looked like we hadn't slept that night. Given how touchy my friend was about my new partner, I didn't want to give him a reason to go off again. Dex was usually a fierce but stable presence at my side, and I didn't know how to deal with this new, angry facet of his personality. It was almost as disconcerting as Frank's sudden disapproval of my actions at every turn.

I dispelled my concerns when Reed and I settled into work, splitting up the names of the customers at Dusk to continue the research I had begun that morning. It was fairly dull work, and I found myself running background checks on each person by rote. All I needed was a name and address to lead me to a social security number, and then I had more than enough information about every person on the list. Sometimes, it scared me to realize how easy it was for me to delve into the lives of strangers, just because of one short string of numbers and the right security clearance.

I pushed aside my moral qualms. Catching The Mentor was more important than my personal feelings of guilt. It didn't take me long to get to the surnames beginning with *C*, and my little shocked gasp popped through the silence.

"What?" Reed asked immediately. "What did you find?"

I gaped at the name and address. Ran it, just to be sure. One hit. *Kennedy Carver.*

"Your boss." I turned disbelieving eyes on him. "Your boss is on this list."

"Oh. I figured he might be." He shrugged and turned back to his work as though what I had found was of no consequence. "You can skip me when you get to the *M*s." He shot me a sardonic grin. "I promise I'm completely innocent."

"Wait," my brain tried to catch up. "You knew Carver is a patron at Dusk?" I remembered Reed's familiarity with Josh Dover. I had suspected that he had visited the club before, and he didn't hide his lifestyle. But his boss?

Reed rolled his eyes. "Could you not shriek it out like that? Kennedy doesn't keep it secret, but that's not exactly common knowledge. I think he tries to keep his more public activities limited to clubs outside New York."

I pitched my voice lower. "So your boss is a Dom. And so are you. And you've both been to Dusk. That's a bit of a small world, isn't it?"

"Not really. There are more of us than you think. We just tend to frequent the same places. Really great clubs are hard to find. Kennedy and I aren't the only lifestylers in the New York unit. And I can promise you I'm not the only one in the Chicago unit now." He shot me a significant look. "Why don't you leave the *S*s to me."

*S*s? *Who does he think-?* Dex. Dexter Scott.

"Or you could hand over the whole list to me."

All the blood drained from my face. It was as though my thoughts had summoned my friend. I craned my head back to find him looming over me, scowling.

"I want in on this," he declared. "Frank might have pulled me from being your partner, but I still want to help with The Mentor case. Let me handle the patrons of Dusk. It's desk work, anyway. You need to go out and speak to Sally Johnson's family."

I winced. I hadn't wanted to face them. We had recently IDed the last of the eight women Martel had murdered, and Sally Johnson had been a Chicago native. Looking further into the activities of the other women before their disappearances, we had found that they all had reason to be in Chicago around the time they were taken. Martel lived outside NYC, but it seemed he had done his hunting here. Lydia Chase had first given the case footing in Chicago, but this new discovery shifted the investigation here more fully. It was one of the reasons Reed had been sent to work with me.

But there was nothing worse than facing a victim's family. Especially in a case like this. The anguish in their eyes when they thought of their daughter or wife being tortured before she was killed was almost too terrible to look upon. Even worse was the dead-eyed stare that so many parents developed in these cases.

*I hate my job.* But my work was important. I would bring to justice the man who was responsible for teaching Martel how to hurt Sally. I could at least give her family that.

Even as I thought it, I knew it was a hollow comfort. Justice was just a word, an idea people used to combat their own sense of frailty, to allow them to pretend that there was some sense of fairness in the world. Justice wouldn't bring back the person they loved. I had learned that the hard way. Watching the man who shot my father being sentenced to life in prison hadn't eased the ache inside my heart.

"I wish I could be there with you." Dex's gentle voice called me back to him. His blue eyes were earnest, concerned. He knew me well enough to know what was going through my head. He had long ago realized how much I hated this part of my work.

"Me too," I said quietly.

Warmth enveloped my hand, and I looked down to find that Reed was gently squeezing my fingers in a show of comfort.

*"I'll be with you,"* his black eyes told me.

Even though he hadn't spoken the words aloud, I still noticed Dex stiffen at my side. He clearly hated my obvious closeness with my new partner. If I didn't know better, I would say his heated glare was one of jealousy.

But Dex didn't think of me like that. Surely he was just being protective of me. Like Frank, Dex didn't approve when men got close to me. Once, I might have been grateful, but now it just made me feel awkward. Because this time, I actually wanted the man who was close to me.

I stood abruptly. "We should go," I announced, not looking at either man. "Thanks for the help, Dex." It truly was a relief to hand over the list from Dusk to him. Seeing his name on it would just be too weird.

Then I thought of where I was headed. I immediately regretted my agreement to leave the desk work to Dex. I would rather do anything else than face Sally Johnson's family.

■■■■■■■■■■■■■■■■■■■■■■■■■■■■■■■■■■■■■■■■■■■■■■■■■■■■■■

I felt as though I had aged ten years in the half hour we spent questioning the Johnsons. Weariness and grief sank all the way into my bones, and I couldn't wait to get up to my apartment and cuddle Gizmo.

We had asked about ex-boyfriends, enemies, or any new acquaintances around the time Sally went missing. The worst part was pressing for information about her sex life. We needed to know if she had been involved in BDSM, but her father had become enraged by my questions, asking if we thought his daughter deserved what happened to her. Reed managed to calm him down, but we left shortly thereafter.

And we hadn't discovered anything new. I had put the Johnsons through hell all over again, and for nothing. I felt like crap. More and more often lately, I found myself longing for the life I had dreamed of when I was younger.

*I should have gone to vet school.*

"I'll walk you up," Reed told me. I blinked and realized that we had pulled up outside my apartment.

"Okay," I agreed before I could process that it probably wasn't a good idea. I had kissed him in my apartment just that morning. Being alone with Reed in a private space was inadvisable. But sexual arousal was the last thing on my mind in that moment, so I deemed it safe. It was only logical that I allow him to see me to my door. I still had a stalker who might be watching me even now.

*Claude Parnell.* I had almost forgotten about him. My weariness sank deeper, and my legs turned leaden as I walked into my building. Out of the corner of my eye, I caught Reed shooting me worried glances, and twice his hand twitched as though to reach out for me. I was relieved that he didn't. I knew I would crumble if he did. I was too tired, too vulnerable. Throwing myself into his arms would have been a sweet relief. It was a relief I couldn't allow myself to indulge in. Reed was my coworker, and while starting a relationship wasn't technically against the rules, it was frowned upon. Frank would do more than frown. He would scowl. And probably find a way to boot Reed out of Chicago.

My brooding ceased when I realized we were standing at the door to my apartment, Reed watching me expectantly. I gave my head a little shake and dug my keys out of my pocket. I inserted them in the lock, then paused as a thought occurred to me.

"You're going to stay outside again, aren't you?" I knew Reed's answer before he spoke.

"Yep." His easy expression hardened in warning. "And don't bother trying to talk me out of it."

I sighed in a show of resignation, but secretly I was pleased for the excuse to keep him close by. "You can stay on the couch. At least you can get some sleep that way."

One corner of his lips tugged up. "Doubtful. I've seen your couch. It's probably two feet too short for me. Besides, I should keep an eye out for Parnell."

"You have to sleep, Reed. If you're worried about my safety, staying inside is just as effective as staying outside. I'll have you nearby as backup either way. Caffeine can only keep you going for so long. You probably have toxic levels in your bloodstream already."

He studied me carefully, his eyes flicking from the sad twist of my mouth to the tired lines around my eyes. "All right," he capitulated after a moment. "You get inside. I'll go grab my spare clothes from the car."

I obeyed and stepped into my safe haven. Gizmo was instantly at my ankles, curling around them and shouting out a chorus of throaty meows. Even through my exhaustion, he drew a little smile from me. I bent down and scooped up his considerable weight. Gizmo was on a diet, but he was still too hefty.

"I know, I know. You're the saddest cat in the world, and you're starving." His yellow eyes were full of reproach at my mocking. He mewed his annoyance, and I laughed for the first time in hours. I showed him my gratitude through giving him too many cat treats, and he quickly forgave me for making fun of his dramatics. By the time Reed returned, I was sitting on the couch in my pajamas, and Gizmo was curled up on my lap, purring.

My partner eyed my furry child warily. "Who's this?"

"This is Gizmo," I introduced. "Gizmo, this is Reed." I expected him to step closer and give my cat a scratch behind the ears, but Reed stood a careful distance away. "What's up?" I asked, confused. Reed struck me as the caring type; I would have thought he loved animals.

"I, uh… I don't really spend any time around animals."

"What?" The concept was utterly foreign to me.

"I didn't have pets growing up, and I've lived in small apartments ever since." Reed shrugged, but to my shock, he looked a bit embarrassed. He didn't take a step closer to us.

Was the big bad Dom really afraid of my cat? I suppressed a giggle. "He won't scratch your or anything. Gizmo's a big softie. Come say hello," I encouraged. If Reed was staying at my apartment, he would have to make friends with the chubby little furball.

He approached slowly and reached out a tentative hand. After a moment, he awkwardly patted Gizmo with the barest touch of his fingertips. This time, I couldn't hold back my snort of amusement. Reed shot me a rueful smile.

"You two will work things out when Gizmo comes to sleep on your chest tonight. He loves invading people's personal space."

To my amazement, Reed almost blanched, and I laughed outright. God, it felt good to laugh. His grin returned at the sound of my levity.

"I'm sure we'll get along just fine."

I was relieved to hear it. It would have been a deal-breaker if Reed hadn't liked my cat.

*A deal-breaker? There is no deal to be broken. He's off-limits, remember?*

My exhaustion seeped back into me, and my good humor melted away. Reed's concern was back.

"You should get some sleep," he told me kindly, but firmly.

"You had better sleep, too. No more caffeine," I ordered. I was seriously concerned that the man would go into shock if he had one more cup of coffee.

"Yes, ma'am." His smile turned sardonic, as though he found my bossiness cute. Heat flared between my legs in response to his cockiness. My cheeks pinkened.

"Goodnight, then." I spoke to the carpet. I couldn't meet his eyes.

"Goodnight, Katie."

I almost fled to my room, and I closed the door behind me. The wood between us wasn't quite thick enough to smother his low chuckle. My sex pulsed at the sound, and I squeezed my thighs together. I threw myself into my bed and drew the covers all the way up over my head, as though I could hide from my arousal and embarrassment.

Despite my consternation, the toll of my difficult day weighed heavily upon me, and I quickly fell into sleep.

# Chapter 8

"Daddy!" I screamed as crimson bloomed across the front of my father's crisp white shirt. His smiling face went oddly slack, and his deep green eyes turned dull. His body sagged forward, and I caught him. He jerked against me in time with the *pops* that rent the air around us. Five hits. Five bullets. But Daddy had already been gone at the first.

His dead weight took me down with him. The strong chest that had once been a place of solace and comfort now crushed me. He was so heavy. I couldn't draw breath. I shoved against him, gasping, but my hands slipped through something slick and hot.

*Blood.*

"Daddy!" I sobbed, but he didn't answer. More sticky heat poured over my fingers.

*Dead.* He was dead. He couldn't hear me. I shrieked out my grief and fear.

"Katie. Wake up." It was a firm order, accompanied by a gentle touch on my shoulder. I jolted awake, twisting away from the stranger. "It's just me. It's Reed." His fingers curled around my upper arm, holding me in place so I couldn't lash out at him.

I blinked and then went so still that even my lungs stopped moving. Reed was indeed the man hovering over me. And he wasn't wearing any clothes. My widened eyes raked over his bare chest. His golden skin rippled over bulging muscles, dusted by dark hair that tapered to a thin line that led downward over his defined abs…

I tore my gaze from his perfection before I reached the part of him I wanted to see most. I gasped air back into my chest.

"You're naked," I exclaimed rather stupidly.

"If you'll stop being squeamish, you'll see that I'm wearing boxers. I promise it's safe to look." His voice held a mocking edge.

"Oh." *Idiot.* Of course he wasn't going to sleep in his work clothes. "Don't you have any pajamas?" The words were somewhere between accusatory and panicked. How was I supposed to resist staring at his ripped body? Especially when he was in my bedroom. Sitting on my bed. So close that I could feel the heat of him. His firm grip on my shoulder suddenly burned, awakening warmth at my core.

He chuckled, and the warmth flared hotter. That dark, arrogant sound just did something for me.

"I wasn't exactly going to change into pajamas in my car. I wasn't planning on this sleepover, remember?"

My eyes flicked to his, before instantly dropping back to his chest. Even in the dim lighting from the streetlamp that filtered through my blinds, I could still see that he was glorious. Shadows gathered in the hollows beneath his muscles. I wanted to trace that darkness with my tongue, to taste its velvety decadence.

Then I noticed the four thin red lines scratched into his chest. "You're bleeding!"

His smile was lopsided, rueful. "Your cat didn't like it when I leapt up to come see what was wrong with you. He did decide to sleep on my chest, after all, and he wasn't pleased when I threw him off." Lines of concern appeared around his eyes "You were crying out, Katie. I was worried Parnell had gotten in somehow. Are you okay?"

*I'm fine,* I wanted to say. I wanted to push it away, ignore it. If I buried it deeply enough, I could overcome it. My grief would fade.

But that was wrong. The loss of my father still crippled me, tormenting me in my sleep when my guard was down. I had never learned to deal with it because I had always buried it.

"No," I whispered the admission. "I'm not okay."

His fingers pressed into my flesh where he still held me down, giving me a little reassuring squeeze. "Tell me about it."

He wasn't asking. And I didn't even think about hesitating.

"My dad," I said softly. "I was dreaming about him."

Reed's expression was soft and full of understanding. "He was killed in the line of duty, right?"

I swallowed and nodded. "He was shot on a drugs raid. I was seventeen."

"Did they catch the man who did it?"

"Yes. He's in prison."

Reed's lips twisted in a mirror of my own pain. "But it doesn't help, does it? Punishing the people who take the ones we love doesn't bring them back."

*Empathy.* I realized Reed had lost someone to violence, too. My hand found his, and I covered his fist with my palm. "No. It doesn't."

"You have these dreams often." Again, it wasn't a question.

"Yes." The temptation to lie, to deflect, was absent. No one ever encouraged me to share my grief. Doing so was a relief. And doing so with Reed felt as natural as breathing. He had made it clear that he would accept nothing less than complete honesty from me, and sharing these hard truths with him was incredibly freeing, if painful. The pain *was* freedom. Freedom to feel, freedom to be vulnerable.

The first sob was cleansing. Strong arms closed around me, and Reed drew my body up against his. He held me as I cried, and I reveled in the warm, solid strength of him. He wanted this from me. He wanted it *for* me. My tears purged the grief from my soul, siphoning some of it off.

When my crying slowed and I could finally breathe normally, I looked up into Reed's kind eyes. "You lost someone, too."

He nodded, and the lines of his face tightened. "My mother. I was fourteen."

"Will it always hurt like this?"

His expression softened again. "The ache in your heart will always be there, because you'll never forget the love you had for your father. That part of your heart belonged to him, and it always will. But if you accept it, if you acknowledge that a piece of you will always be his even though he's gone, you can learn to live with it. You can heal the ragged edges around the hole in your heart." He cupped my cheek, and his thumb gently brushed away the wetness there. "Pain can be good, Katie. You don't have to fight it. Accepting it can bring release."

The way his eyes darkened let me know that he wasn't talking about just emotional pain anymore. "Is that why you're into BDSM? I didn't think Doms took pain."

His lips quirked up at the corners; he was evidently pleased that I had followed his line of thinking. "I don't. I find my release in control. But more importantly, I find it in trust. A submissive has to have complete trust in me for her to allow me to give her pain." He paused. "Do you trust me, Katie?"

Yearning rose up in me. "I trust you. And I want that." Yes, I wanted Reed. And I wanted the pain he could give me. I longed to find the release he promised. Desire licked between my thighs at the idea of him dominating my body, allowing me to give in to my darkest fantasies.

Fear of what wanting pain with sex meant tickled at the edges of my mind, but all my focus was honed on Reed. *Wrong,* a little voice warned. I shouldn't be with Reed. But the entirety of the rest of my being burned for him, in a way that was so much more than physical desire. Although that was quite potent enough.

I became acutely aware of everywhere his skin touched mine. My side was pressed against his chest, and his arms surrounded me. His muscles coiled, tightening around me, trapping me. My head dropped back, and I went soft in his hold.

His triumphant grin gleamed through the darkness, and his hand slid up my back to grip my nape. I shuddered at the dominant touch, and the sparse light in the room gathered in his eyes, flashing across the inky surface like fireworks across the night sky.

His lips were still curved up with his pleasure when they descended on mine. I opened for him, and his mouth claimed me. His kiss was every bit as heady as I remembered. My mind had tried to push away memories of the pleasure of it. If I could deny how good his touch upon me felt, I could resist him. But Reed demanded honesty, and he had ripped away my ability to lie even to myself. I moaned up into him, releasing my lust just as I had released my grief in his arms. The shot of freedom was almost as intoxicating as his lips moving against mine.

Keeping one hand cradling the back of my neck, his other found the top button of my pajamas. It suddenly struck me that they were bright pink and patterned with cartoon dogs and cats. I burned with embarrassment, but Reed didn't seem to mind. He deftly slid the button free and slipped inside the soft fabric. The sensation of his calloused fingertips against my smooth skin sent a shiver racing up my spine. There was nothing tentative about his touch, no silent hesitation waiting for my permission. His fingers explored the expanse of creamy flesh as though he had every right.

My nipples pebbled, aching for him. He obliged my need. Pain bloomed as he pinched one between his thumb and forefinger. He caught my little cry on his tongue, consuming it. Mercilessly, he twisted, pulling and pinching. I tried to move away from him, but I was caught between his hand on my neck and his mouth upon mine. His teeth sank into my lower lip, reinforcing my utter helplessness to resist him. His grip shifted to torture my other nipple. I shuddered and surrendered to the pain, acknowledging it rather than fighting or denying it.

With my acceptance, the pain became something more, something *interesting.* It didn't stop hurting, but the burning in my breast awoke an answering burn in my belly. Pleasure bloomed along with my submission, weaving through the pain in an exquisite symphony of sensation. I squirmed in Reed's lap, seeking stimulation against my throbbing clit. He hardened beneath me in response, and I let out a little gasp at the size of him. Even as I registered trepidation at the idea of taking a man so large, my inner walls contracted, longing to be filled. A strange whine eased up my throat as carnal need overtook my mind.

Abruptly, Reed moved my body. The world spun around me, and then I found myself lying flat on my back. He grasped my wrists and drew them up over my head. His hands found mine, and his thumbs pressed against my palms, forcing them to unfurl. Then his touch shifted, urging my fingers to close to fists. They wrapped around something cool and smooth: one of the wooden slats on my headboard.

His lips left mine to utter one low word in my ear. "Stay."

His weight lifted from me, and my eyes widened when he turned to leave the room. I almost asked him where he was going, but I kept the question pressed between my lips. He wouldn't have told me to stay in this position if he wasn't coming back. Surely not. The smirk he shot back at me just before he disappeared through my open door reassured me that he would return. And that he had something wicked planned for me.

My fingers trembled, and I gripped the bed tighter to still them.

Reed returned seconds later, and I sucked in a breath when his body created a hulking silhouette against the light from the window. Although he was the one whose skin was exposed, he radiated more authority than he did in his sharp suit, and I felt naked and vulnerable under his dark stare.

He closed the distance between us slowly, wrapping something through his fist as he approached. His thin black tie dangled from his other hand. In the sensual darkness, it became something more menacing than a simple article of clothing. And the way Reed prowled toward me only added to the sense of danger.

Despite the little zing of fear elicited by the perceived threat, I remained where he had positioned me. My decision not to act, the knowledge that I was willingly sacrificing my body, just got me hotter for him.

His weight settled over me again, and I groaned at the sensation of being pinned by him. His cocky laugh tickled across my neck. Silken fabric looped over my wrists. When it tightened around them, my sex squeezed in response. My breath began to come in little pants as I registered the fact that I was restrained, powerless to resist whatever Reed wanted to do to me. My arousal was a sweet pain. Desperation overtook me, and I arched up against him. His chuckle vibrated through his lips when he pressed them against my collarbone. His tongue traced a hot line down to the hollow between my breasts as his fingers found the second button to my pajama top. I no longer cared that the pattern on them might seem juvenile; all I cared about was Reed taking them off, baring my body to him. I craved to feel his skin against mine.

The soft material of my shirt teased across my nipples as he slowly parted the fabric, sliding it over my breasts. The cool air that swept over my exposed skin was quickly chased away by his heat. His fingers traced a circular pattern around my areolae, and the dark pools of his eyes deepened with hunger as he watched my nipples tighten. He lowered his head and brushed a feather-light kiss over each of them, teasing me.

"Beautiful," he breathed just before his teeth closed around one of the hardened buds. I cried out, but my body arched up into the pain rather than pulling away. He released me in reward, and his tongue eased the lingering sting of his bite. Pleasure rolled through me, shooting from my nipple in a hot line that ran straight to my clit.

I rocked my hips up against him, and my pleasure increased when I rubbed against his hard cock.

"Please, Reed," I whispered.

His lips took on a cruelly amused twist, and his eyes sparkled. "Please, what? Tell me what you want, Katie." His hips rotated, grinding his cock directly against my clit.

I gasped out my need. "I want…" I trailed off, biting my lip. Instead of saying something embarrassing, I rubbed up against him again.

He moved away from me, settling back on heels. His knees pressed my thighs apart, spreading me wide.

"You want more pain," he told me coolly. "I'll give it to you, Katie. I'll teach you to beg me to fuck you without hesitation."

My protest stuck in my throat. Even as instinct told me to fight his promise of pain, my body burned for it. He was right; I wasn't ready to beg him to *fuck me*. I had never said anything so crass in bed. Sex with George had been a rather silent, rote affair. I had never *wanted* to beg anyone to fuck me. Reed was about to change that.

His hands fisted in my pajama pants, jerking them down and exposing me with one powerful move of his arms. It felt as though he was stripping away more than my clothes. He was stripping away the last barriers between us, the last of my defenses.

He watched me carefully as he began to uncoil the object that was still wrapped around his fist. Silver flashed, and I recognized his belt buckle. By the time he held the length of black leather doubled over in his hand, my breath came in short, shallow gasps.

"Reed…" My voice wavered as uncertainty coiled within my gut.

White hot pain exploded across my sensitive inner thigh, and I shrieked in shock.

"You will address me as 'Sir,'" he ordered calmly. "If you want me to stop, say 'red.' Otherwise, this won't end until you beg me to fuck you. 'No' and 'stop' aren't safe words."

My whimper was a mixture of fear and desire. He took it as an invitation to continue. His belt slapped me again, mirroring the first hit. The pain was hot, stinging. It pulsed across my skin until it found my sex, where it turned to an erotic throb. My core clenched at the third hit, even as my body tried to jerk away from him. But his knees held me open for his torment, and his tie kept my hands securely restrained. The knowledge of my helplessness only increased my desire for him.

"Please!" I shouted out at the fourth blow. "Please. F-fuck me." I stumbled over the word.

"Not good enough." His voice was merciless, and the belt came down again.

"Please fuck me, Reed!" I didn't hesitate this time.

Hot pain lashed me. "Try again."

"Please, Sir," I gasped, realizing what he wanted. "Please fuck me." All embarrassment or insecurity had been melted by the heat of his belt against my sensitive thighs, leaving nothing but need and lust behind. Just as Reed had promised, pain had brought me release. Now I needed a different sort of release. "Please fuck me, Sir." My hips lifted toward him, silently begging.

"Come for me first." As soon as he uttered the words, he brought the belt down directly on my swollen clit. Sensation exploded across the tiny bundle of nerves. I wasn't sure if it was pleasure or pain. They were one in the same, a purely carnal feeling that ripped through me with blinding force. My sharp cry barely registered in my ears.

His fingers brushed against the abused bud, and I twisted against my bonds as sensation flooded me mercilessly. Was this an orgasm? I had thought I had found pleasure with my vibrator, but that was nothing compared to this bliss.

It wasn't until I was quivering and utterly spent that his touch left me. I heard the rustling of fabric, and the way the mattress shifted let me know he was removing his boxers. I blinked against the white light that flooded my vision, yearning to see him. His strong form coalesced in the darkness just as he sheathed himself in a condom. Then his huge cock was at my entrance. I nearly protested. No way would he fit. But somehow, there was still a burn within me, a deeper need that hadn't been fulfilled by the pleasure he had just given me. I needed *him.*

His eyes met mine, trapping me in his bottomless gaze. Two fluttering heartbeats passed, and then he drove into me in one thrust. The double-edged sword of pain/pleasure impaled me once again as he stretched me ruthlessly. He stilled, holding himself deep within me.

"Fuck., you're tight." He drew in sharp breaths through his teeth as he restrained himself from fucking me with the ferocity he clearly desired. My tightness was causing him his own sweet pain. His hands cupped my face, his thumbs hooking below my jaw to tilt my head back. My lips parted, and his tongue invaded my mouth, stroking against mine as his cock would rub against my inner walls. Arousal caused me to clench around him, and he hissed out his own pleasure. I relaxed, my body welcoming him, and he began to move within me. He started slowly so as not to damage me, but his pace increased as I softened to accommodate him.

The head of his cock found a sweet spot inside me, and my eyes flew wide as I cried out in shocked pleasure. He altered the angle of his hips and made contact with it again. He groaned as my muscles fluttered around him.

"Again, Katie. Come for me." He fucked me in earnest, rubbing against my g-spot. I flew apart with a sharp scream. He caught it on his lips, and he groaned his own orgasm into my mouth. Our pleasure mingled, amplifying our bliss as we found completion in one another. It was the most intimate thing I had ever experienced. And I had found it through complete surrender.

When Reed finally withdrew from me, I felt almost delirious, drunk on the high he had given me. He released my wrists and planted gentle kisses on the grooves left in my skin by his tie.  He eased down on the mattress beside me, and my body curled around his.  Before I realized what was happening, I fell asleep in his arms.

# Chapter 9

"Shit. Katie, wake up. We're going to be late."

I groaned my protest. I hated waking up early. And it had to be early, because I felt like I was being ripped out of the deepest sleep. The mattress shifted as someone rolled away from me.

"I'm getting a shower. You'd better be up by the time I'm out. You have five more minutes, Sleeping Beauty." A whisper-soft kiss brushed against my forehead.

*Wait. What?*

My eyes fluttered open just in time to see Reed's perfectly sculpted ass before he shut the bathroom door.

*Holy. Shit.*

Reed was naked. And he had just gotten out of my bed. Where we had slept together. After *sleeping together.*

This time, my groan was one of dread. I pulled my covers up over my head, as though I could hide from what I had done. I had sex with a coworker. I had sex with my partner.

No, that wasn't right. Reed had *fucked me.* After I begged him to. After he had tied me down and whipped me with his belt. My sex burned as hot as my cheeks at the memory. I pressed my thighs together, and a little twinge of pain reminded me of how sweet the pain he had given me had been.

How could I possibly be anywhere near him without wanting him? Would I fall to my knees in the middle of the office every time he turned that dark stare on me? He had stripped me bare, made me vulnerable. And I had loved every delicious second of my submission to him. It had been so much more than just a physical connection. I had cried in his arms before he brought me pleasure.

*This can't happen.* I couldn't be with Reed. It wasn't appropriate. It wasn't professional.

Oh, god, how was I going to face Dex? And worse, Frank? I shuddered to think what would happen to Reed if my father figure found out I had slept with him. Best case scenario, he would be shipped back to New York. I didn't even want to contemplate the worst case scenario. It probably involved a lot of pain for Reed.

"Time's up." I registered the amusement in his voice just before the comforter was ripped away from me, leaving my naked body exposed. With a surprised squeak, I covered myself as best I could with my hands.

Reed grinned down at me. He was wearing nothing but a towel slung low on his hips, and it tented with his growing erection. "You're awfully shy this morning," he remarked with amusement.

Frantically, I searched for something to hide my nakedness from his dancing eyes. I found my crumpled pajama top and hastily draped it over my front. Reed's grin widened, as though he found my efforts immensely funny. I tore my gaze from his mocking one and scrambled off the bed, making my way to the bathroom.

He let out a low, satisfied rumble. "The view's just as nice from the back."

His hand cracked across my ass as I passed him. I jolted forward, practically leaping into the bathroom in three long strides. His laugh filtered through the door even after I closed it behind me. I took a deep breath as I leaned against it. How was I going to make it through the day without blushing every time he looked at me?

The solution was both simple and familiar: ignore it. I would throw myself into my work and forget the night of passion I had shared with Reed. The prospect of forgetting made me sick with regret, but it was my only option. I had a job to do, and I couldn't do it properly if I wasn't able to think of anything but my sexy partner. Catching The Mentor was more important than my newfound ecstasy at the hands of Reed Miller.

■■■■■■■■■■■■■■■■■■■■■■■■■■■■■■■■■■■■■■■■■■■■■■■■■■■■■■■■

"Are you always this miserable in the morning?" Reed asked as we rode the elevator up to the office. His playful joy had turned to consternation in the wake of my obvious discontent.

"I didn't get enough sleep last night," I said before I realized the implications.

"Sorry about that." Reed's smile wasn't remotely repentant.

I pursed my lips and made a careful study of the dirty carpet. I could practically feel his pleasure deflate.

"What's wrong, Katie?"

"Nothing," I lied.

"Katie-"

I strode out of the open elevator doors before he could issue a warning for my dishonesty. I had been honest with him the night before, and look where that had gotten me. Into a clusterfuck, that's where.

"I'm going to check my emails," I tossed back over my shoulder. *I need a few minutes away from you.*

He didn't acknowledge my unspoken desire for him to give me some space. I decided to pretend he wasn't hovering just behind me. He couldn't turn his inner Dom on me in the middle of the office. Oh, god, I hoped he wouldn't.

His presence was a disapproving menace at my back as I sat on the edge of my chair in front of my desk. My fingers trembled as I turned on my computer. Just before the monitor turned blue, I caught his angry reflection in the black screen.

*I am in so much trouble.* Ignoring Reed wasn't going to work. I should have known better than that. What would I have to do to make him forget last night had ever happened? To at least get him to pretend like it had never happened?

I blew out a long breath. "Reed-" I wasn't sure what I was going to say, but my thought processes were cut off by a sharp cry. My attention snapped back to my computer. It took two horrible seconds for what I was seeing to sink in. The image was rendered in black and green, as though the scene were being watched through night vision. A woman was restrained, tied to her bed. A man knelt between her knees. He brought his belt down across her thighs, and she screamed again.

*"I knew you enjoyed pain, Kathy,"* a distorted voice emanated from my computer. *"You were made for me. Come and find me."*

A loud error noise made me jump, and the screen went black.

"Fuck." Reed reached around me and started fiddling with the keyboard, but the computer didn't respond. I stared at the blank screen, taking in my reflection. It looked so much paler in the light than it had in green and black. "We need to get someone from tech up here now. We have to trace this," Reed said. The screen remained unresponsive, and the usual soft whir of the computer was absent. Distantly, I listened to Reed making a hurried phone call to the tech department. I edged away from him.

I closed my eyes, wishing that when I opened them everything would go away. But that was a childish wish.

"What's going on?" Dex's voice rumbled behind me.

I couldn't even begin to find the words to describe the awfulness of what I had just seen. What was I going to say? *"A video clip of Reed whipping me just showed up on my computer"*?

"There are cameras in Katie's apartment," Reed practically snarled. "Parnell just sent a clip of her in her bedroom, and now the fucking computer's crashed."

"I heard screaming," Dex said.

*"I knew you enjoyed pain, Kathy."* I wanted to vomit. I had known it was wrong to want pain with sex, but Reed had made me forget that. He had made it seem natural, blissful.

"There was a voiceover," Reed misdirected. "The same as before: *'Come and find me.'* We have to go back to her apartment and-"

"Go back?" Dex asked sharply. "As in, you were just there?"

"I drove Katie to work this morning." It wasn't a lie, but Reed managed to sidestep the truth. At least he was trying to keep it secret. It wouldn't stay secret for long once tech got their hands on my computer.

*"You were made for me."*

"Katie?" Reed's hand came down on my shoulder in a show of concern, but I jolted away from him with a little yelp.

His brow furrowed, and he reached for me again. I jumped to my feet and backed away as though retreating from a stalking predator. My back came into contact with something solid, and I whirled.

Dex caught my upper arms in his large hands, steadying me. His blue eyes were accusatory. I jerked out of his hold.

"I need some air," I managed to say. Reed stepped forward to follow me, and I shot him a warning look. *"Alone."*

His handsome features twisted into a grimace, and his outstretched hand clenched to a fist. He gave me a single, short nod. His disapproval was palpable, but he wasn't going to push me. Not now.

I tried my best to draw in regular, even breaths as I strode back toward the elevator. I was seconds away from being blessedly alone in the small space when Dex slipped through the closing silver doors.

"What part of *alone* don't you understand?" I snapped.

His gorgeous face was a thunderhead. "You slept with him."

I blanched. Oh, god. This was the last thing I wanted to deal with right now. I pressed my palm to my forehead, as though I could shove all the horror out of my brain.

"I can't do this right now, Dex."

"All this time, I resisted. I thought you wouldn't understand."

"What are you talking about?" I snapped.

His fingers closed around my wrist, gently pulling my hand away from my face. I lifted my eyes to find his burning down into me with a fervor I had never seen before.

"I'm talking about *you*, Katie. I'm talking about the fucked up shit we see every day. You're always so disgusted by sexual violence; I thought you would never understand what I wanted from you."

My head started shaking of its own accord. "No. Dex-"

He gripped my chin between his thumb and forefinger, stilling my physical sign of denial. "Yes. You're going to listen to me, Sparrow. All this time, I haven't touched you because I thought you couldn't handle it. I thought if I went slow enough, you would realize you're submissive. And now *he's* come in and-"

"Dex! Stop. Please, stop." I couldn't handle this.

"No. I fucking love you, Katie. I've always loved you. You can't-"

But whatever it was I couldn't do was cut off by the sound of my hand cracking across his cheek. His grip on my face loosened with his shock, and I jerked away from him with a sob.

"I'm sorry," I gasped out, horrified. It was too much all at once. My uncertainty at having slept with Reed, the disgusting realization that my stalker had witnessed the most intimate moments of my life, and now the revelation that I had just betrayed my best friend without realizing it… "God, Dex. I'm so sorry." I was apologizing for so much more than hitting him.

The elevator doors slid open, and I flung myself out into the parking garage. I was grateful that Dex didn't stop me. I ran to my car and locked myself inside. All I wanted to do was break down and cry out my painful emotions like Reed had shown me, but that wasn't an option. If I stayed, he would come looking for me. Or Dex would. I wasn't sure which was worse.

I harnessed my fear and anguish and shoved them down. Tears spilled over my cheeks, but I managed to keep my vision clear enough to drive away from the two men who were tearing my heart apart. I pealed out of the parking garage and disappeared into the city.

∎∎∎∎∎∎∎∎∎∎∎∎∎∎∎∎∎∎∎∎∎∎∎∎∎∎∎∎∎∎∎∎∎∎∎∎∎∎∎∎∎∎∎∎∎∎∎∎∎∎∎∎∎∎

I parked at my apartment and then took the subway to Michigan Avenue. I spent hours wandering aimlessly, as though I could leave my feelings behind if I just walked far enough. It was almost a relief when darkness began to fall. At least this hellish day would be over.

Then I remembered that I couldn't go back to my apartment, and my anguish bubbled up all over again. I knew I would have to go back and face everything soon, but I wasn't ready. Reed had called and texted dozens of times. Finally, I had texted him that I needed some time alone and switched my phone to silent mode. The quiet was merciful. I hadn't gone this long without getting a call from work in years. If they really needed me, the phone had GPS tracking. I wasn't going back to face the guys at the office short of being hauled in against my will. I was being stalked. Surely Frank wouldn't begrudge me the day off.

And it wasn't as though I was being stupid. I stayed in public areas, always within sight of other people. Even if I was being watched by Parnell, he couldn't do anything to me in broad daylight.

But it wouldn't be daylight for much longer. With a sigh, I realized it was time for me to get a hotel room. I wouldn't be able to sleep, but at least I could hole up for the night and avoid reality for a few hours longer.

I cut through the Park District, making my way to the Palmer House. After the day I'd had, I could treat myself to four-star luxury. The woman at the check-in desk was generically friendly, and I went through the motions of handing over my credit card without wincing at the price. She told me my room number, and I slowly made my way to the elevators, wishing I had a change of clothes. Getting off my feet after walking all day would have to be comfort enough.

As soon as the door to my room clicked closed behind me, a large, hard body hit me from the side. Something sharp pierced my neck, and my shocked cry was smothered by a gloved hand. I tried to lash out, but the weight of the person behind me slammed me forward against the wall, stunning me. My muscles started to go strangely watery, and a black cloth slipped down over my eyes.

"Down you go, Kathy." Fear stabbed through me at the low, gravelly words. My scream might have been loud enough to escape the hand against my mouth, but my voice was weak, and barely more than a whine escaped me. My entire body felt too light, as though I would float away if it weren't for the man's arms wrapped around me, easing me down to the plush carpet.

He positioned me on my back, and his weight settled over me. I tried to lift my arms to lash out at him, but they were too heavy.

*Drugged,* my mind registered with an almost detached horror.

His hands encircled my wrists, drawing my arms up over my head and securing them there so that I was stretched out beneath him. I couldn't help but be reminded of how Reed had positioned me the night before, and I shuddered in revulsion. I tugged against his hold. It was a weak, pathetic gesture.

"Let me go." My demand was low and garbled, almost unintelligible as I shoved the words past my too-thick tongue.

"Shhh, Kathy. You can't fight me. You'll learn that one day." Gloved fingers brushed my cheek. "Although I'll enjoy our time together until then."

Through the nausea that swirled within me, I registered that there was something wrong with his voice. It was far too low and rough to be his natural speaking voice. And he reeked of too much cologne. The man was smart; he wasn't giving me any clues to figure out his identity. With my hands secured and my eyes blindfolded, I had no means of learning more about him through sight or touch. If I ever made it out of this, I wouldn't be able to ID him.

His nose skimmed along my jawline, as though he was sampling the smell of my fear. He groaned out his pleasure, and something hard jerked against my hip.

*His cock.*

I gagged and tried to pull free of his hold, but my muscles barely twitched. The edges of my mind were beginning to go hazy as the drug he had injected me with affected my thought processes. Only adrenaline kept me conscious.

"This is how I'll keep you," his hand tightened around my limp wrists. "Restrained, blind. You'll look to me for everything; food, cleanliness, pleasure. You'll come to love me."

"You're insane," I managed two slurred, terrified words.

His dark laugh oozed over me. "Oh yes, pet. I'm insane. And you're very brave. That makes me… happy." He sighed the word, as though it both surprised and relieved him.

One hand skimmed down my side to find the hem of my shirt. The leather of his gloves was cool and slick across my bare skin as his touch glided up my stomach, snaking beneath my bra to find my breast. A small, unintelligible protest teased at the back of my throat. Cognizant thought gave way to primal panic, but my body was incapable of fight or flight.

"You haven't learned yet, but you belong to me. You let him touch you. You'll be punished for that." His fingers closed around my nipple and twisted cruelly. A sound of pure fear choked up from my chest, and he chuckled against my neck. His cock jerked against my belly in lustful delight.

"But not yet," he continued. "You're going to come to me. I'll even leave you a clue." He squeezed my breast. "I could take you any time I wanted. I could take you right now. But that wouldn't be any fun, would it?"

Something buzzed against my hip. My confused mind couldn't work out what was happening. All I knew was terror and disgust and powerlessness.

"I have to go," he told me regretfully. "But I'll see you soon. Come and find me, my brave little pet."

His heat dissipated, leaving me cold and immobilized and terrified.

# Chapter 10

*Get up! Run!* His heat had left me, but that didn't mean he was gone. Through the haze in my mind, I knew he was enjoying toying with me. This could just be a cruel game, a trick to make me think the threat was truly over. I had to get out of this room. It was too private. It could be hours before anyone found me.

Lethargy sapped my muscles, and although my arms twitched to push myself up, they remained uselessly stretched above my head.

*"This is how I'll keep you. Restrained, blind."*

Panic continued to swirl through the drugs. It was the only thing keeping me awake, but reality was becoming harder and harder to hold on to. I couldn't remember what was happening to me; I only knew I was afraid.

*I can't see. I can't see.* It would be so much easier to just give in to that blackness and fall asleep.

"Katie!" There was a pounding noise, and a small cry of fear escaped me. "Katie!"

*No!* He hadn't left. He was still here, waiting to torment me, to touch me... I gagged and managed to roll onto my side and push up on one elbow for leverage. I had to get away.

There was a loud *bang,* accompanied by the sound of splintering wood. Strong hands closed around my shoulders, and I went tumbling back down. Terror suffused my addled mind, consuming all my senses. Fear was the darkness before my eyes, the metallic taste at the back of my throat.

"Katie!" The hands shook me. Light seared my eyes when the cloth was lifted from them. It hurt, and my lids were so heavy. Temptation to fall into the waiting blackness almost overcame me. Coherent thought was beyond my capability, but I knew I couldn't let myself go. I couldn't make myself vulnerable to my attacker.

"Fuck!" He was holding a syringe, studying it. A strangled whine eased around my thick tongue. I couldn't let him give me more drugs. But my muscles didn't so much as ripple with my need to escape.

He tucked the syringe in his pocket, and his arms closed around me, lifting me up.

*I could take you any time I wanted. I could take you right now.*

"It's okay, Katie. You're going to be okay. I'm getting you to the hospital. Just stay awake for me."

I blinked, forced my eyes to focus.

*Reed.* Reed was carrying me.

My eyes closed without a thought, and I gave myself over to him. Instinct told me Reed meant safety. I didn't have to fight anymore.

His arms tightened around me. "Damn it, Katie," he almost growled. "Open your eyes."

I couldn't obey. With the threat gone, the adrenaline in my system had run its course. I would have been weakened and exhausted under normal circumstances. But with the drugs in my system, I was unable to resist the beguiling peace they offered. I was dimly aware of Reed's curses as I gave in to the silent darkness.

■■■■■■■■■■■■■■■■■■■■■■■■■■■■■■■■■■■■■■■■■■■■■■■■■

I didn't drink often, but I must have really gone for it the night before, because I had a wicked hangover. My head pounded, and my mouth was cotton-dry. My soft pillow felt like a stone against my tender skull. I let out a soft groan and struggled to recall what the hell I had done to myself.

"Katie," my name was a hoarse utterance. He cleared his throat. "Here. Drink some water."

A straw slipped between my chapped lips, and I greedily sucked in the blessedly cool liquid. After three long pulls, a wave of nausea rolled over me, and I turned my head away.

"You'll be okay. The doctor said the discomfort will go away in a few hours. You just have to get hydrated."

*The doctor?* The straw was back at my lips, but I opened my eyes rather than my mouth. I blinked against the pain of harsh, sterile light. Reed was hovering over me, his handsome features taut with concern.

"Drink," he insisted in that dark voice of his. My lips parted, and I forced down more water. It made my stomach turn, but it was a relief to my parched tongue.

I looked past Reed and was shocked to find that I was lying in a hospital bed, with an IV stuck in my arm.

"What happened?" I croaked. I didn't remember getting injured...

*"You haven't learned yet, but you belong to me."*

I retched and only barely managed to keep down the water I had just drunk as pieces of horrific memories coalesced in my mind. My stalker had found me. I had put myself in a vulnerable position for less than a minute, and he had been ready to act. It was stupid of me to stay out alone.

*Blindfolded, held down. The sickly sweet smell of him, the gravelly voice that uttered such sickening words...*

My skin crawled where he had touched me. I shuddered and hugged my arms across my chest, covering my breasts as though I could protect my more vulnerable areas from the memory of him.

"Hey," Reed's voice was gentle, but it held the barest edge of anger. "You're all right. It's over." His arms closed around me, and I buried my face in his chest. I breathed him in, washing away the stench of too much cologne with his rich, salty scent. My exhale left me on a soft sob. He let me cry against him. His strength was a bulwark against the disgusting memories, but the quiet rage I detected in the tightness of his muscles was a subtle reminder that I had been violated.

"I need you to tell me what happened," he said softly when my cries had quieted. I tensed in his arms, but he gave me a reassuring squeeze before he pulled back slightly. His hands remained around my shoulders, tethering me to him, and he fixed me in his earnest black stare. "I know it's difficult to face, but it'll be easier if you get it out now. I need to know so I can catch this fucker, but you need to tell me so that it won't haunt you. Let me help you. Trust me." His lips softened with something akin to yearning at the last.

"I do trust you, Reed. But I don't know if I…" I swallowed hard. "I don't want to talk about it."

His expression turned stern. "Don't bury this, Katie. You know that won't solve anything. It won't help you deal with it, and it won't help us catch Parnell."

*Parnell.* Reed said the sadistic bastard's name as though he was certain of my stalker's identity. I wasn't so sure. I wasn't sure of anything. And that was exactly how my attacker had intended it.

"I don't know, Reed. There's nothing to tell. He caught me off guard and hit me with the drugs, then blindfolded me. I couldn't see him or touch him. He disguised his voice, and he was wearing a ton of cologne to mask his scent. He wore gloves. I can't give you anything that would help you ID him."

"That's helpful, Katie," Reed encouraged me. I gave him a dubious look. "That tells me he's intelligent, and he knows how to counter your training. He's familiar with investigative techniques. He's probably a repeat offender, which further points us toward Parnell. We'll track him down, Katie."

I shook my head. "I don't know. It didn't seem like Parnell. He hates me. The man who attacked me seems to…" I struggled to find the right words. "He doesn't just want to hurt me.

He wants to *keep* me. He said… He said he would make me love him."

Reed didn't seem to realize that his fingers were digging into my flesh. I welcomed the little bite of pain. It kept me grounded in the present.

"I swear I'm going to find him, Katie." A fervent light gleamed across his dark eyes.

I shook my head. "He wants *me* to find him. I don't know what to do, Reed. He said he could take me at any time. And obviously, that's true." I shivered at the knowledge of how easily he could have abducted me. I forced my mind to go into work mode, to analyze my attacker as though he was an ordinary suspect. "He's arrogant. He gets off on seeing what he can get away with. If I don't find him, he'll just keep coming for me. But if I go after him, I'm giving him what he wants." Something occurred to me. "I think he knew you were coming. He left right before you arrived. How would he know that?"

"I don't know, Katie, but we'll look into it. The first thing we have to do is find Parnell. If it's not him, at least we can rule him out once we question him. He might just be saying he wants to keep you in order to scare you. If he does hate you, that would make sense. Especially if he's smart enough to throw you off from IDing him. He could be misrepresenting his intentions as well."

I knew deep in my bones that Reed was wrong. "No," I said quietly. "My attacker wasn't lying. He says I *belong* to him. He keeps calling me his pet."

"Did he touch you?" The barely contained rage in Reed's voice let me know he was asking about more than just my stalker's hands around my wrists.

I looked away, unable to meet his eyes. "Not really."

He cupped my cheek in his hand and firmly turned my face back to his so that his eyes could burn into mine. "Did he touch you?" He wasn't going to tolerate my evasiveness.

"He reached under my shirt," I heard myself whisper. "But he was wearing gloves. He didn't really…" I trailed off. The denial sounded desperate in my own ears.

*"You let him touch you. You'll be punished for that. But not yet,"* he had said. He had twisted my nipple, but that wasn't my punishment. The way his cock had jerked against me let me know he had so much more planned for me.

"Yes," I admitted. "He touched me."

Saying it aloud made it so much more real. It made it so much worse. I tore my eyes from Reed's and gasped in a breath, pushing the horror away. "He said he would leave me a clue," my mind searched for something else to focus on. "Did you find anything?"

Reed's lips thinned, but he allowed the subject change. The harsh grip of his fingers on my arms let me know that he didn't want to think about it, either.

"The syringe. I sent it to forensics for immediate processing. They should be able to let us know what drugs he gave you. I also turned in the blindfold. There might be trace DNA in the fabric; skin cells, hair. If not, they can analyze the fibers for the source of the cloth. Anything they find will help."

"Good," it took all my determination to sound like a detached professional. "That's good." Even though I had only been awake for a few minutes, exhaustion sank into my bones. "I want to go home," I said, my voice small.

Reed's fingers stroked through my hair. "I'm sorry, Katie, but you can't go home. I swept it for bugs today. He's been watching you at your apartment. He knows where you live and how to get in. You're going to stay at my hotel. I'm not letting you out of my sight until we bring this guy down."

I shouldn't have been surprised that he had a plan in place, and that it involved keeping me close. I wasn't sure how I felt about that. Not after the fresh reminders that pain with sex was sick and wrong. Not after Dex had told me he loved me and the implications that he wanted to be my Dom.

I opened my mouth to protest, but nothing came out. I had nowhere else to go. I certainly couldn't stay with Dex, and I wasn't willing to run to Frank like a frightened child. Reed might be showing me how to open myself to my vulnerability, but I was too worried about making Frank disappointed in me by showing weakness. I was supposed to be a strong, competent FBI agent, not a weeping little girl.

"Okay," I agreed, utterly defeated. "I'll stay with you, Reed."

∎∎∎∎∎∎∎∎∎∎∎∎∎∎∎∎∎∎∎∎∎∎∎∎∎∎∎∎∎∎∎∎∎∎∎∎∎∎∎∎∎∎∎∎∎∎∎∎∎∎

"Gizmo!" I dropped to my knees just inside the hotel room door, and my cat leapt into my arms. He gave a sad little meow at having been kidnapped and taken to a strange place without me. I turned watery eyes on Reed. "You brought him here?" I was deeply touched that he hadn't left Gizzy alone.

He gave me his first genuine grin since I had awoken in the hospital. "Yep. And I have the scratches to prove it. He wasn't too keen to get in the box."

The laugh that bubbled up my throat caught me by surprise. "Yeah, he hates leaving my apartment. It usually means he's going to the vet." I cuddled Gizmo closer, and my voice dropped to the silly baby tone I used only with him. "Did big bad Reed scare you?"

Reed snorted. "*Big bad Reed*? Really? I guess I don't hate that. Although I'd prefer if you didn't say it in that crazy cat lady voice."

I flushed at being caught talking to Gizmo. I didn't usually do it in front of other people. "Sorry," I mumbled.

He chuckled. I loved that warm, cocky sound. "There's no need to be sorry. It's kind of cute. Besides, Gizmo and I are friends now." He crouched down beside us and scratched the cat behind the ears. Gizmo closed his eyes and purred.

My brows lifted. "How did you manage that?"

"I gave him lots of cat treats."

I slapped him on the arm. "Gizmo's on a diet!" I scolded.

Reed shrugged. "Doesn't look like it. How was I to know? Besides," he gave me a slow grin, "I like to pamper my pets."

Any warmth I might have felt at this heated stare was doused by the word. My eyes found a spot on the floor just beside Reed's knees. "Don't say that," I whispered. I knew he had been talking about more than Gizmo. And while I might have once found it hot that he was referring to me as a cherished possession, now it left me cold.

*"Come and find me, my brave little pet."*

He let out a low curse. "Sorry, Katie. I didn't mean it like that."

My eyes snapped up to turn an accusatory stare on him. "Didn't you?"

His jaw set. "Okay. I did mean it like that. But I didn't mean to upset you. Do you know how angry it makes me that he's fucking with your mind like this? Don't think I can't see that you're putting your walls back up. Don't let him win, Katie. Don't let him make you deny who you are."

I jumped to my feet, dropping Gizmo. My eyes narrowed. "You don't know me, Reed Miller. You just met me a few days ago. You don't know the first thing about me."

He stood as well, and he suddenly towered over me. "I know you're funny and sweet and have a gentle heart. I know you pretend you're a hard-ass because you feel like you can't show your vulnerability. And I know you're desperate to drop that act and just be yourself. What I don't know is why you won't." He fixed me with a level stare. "Your stalker is counting on you keeping your walls up. He wants you to stay isolated, untrusting. That's what makes you vulnerable, Katie, not your emotions."

Anger boiled up. It was so much easier than the fear I felt at how easily he had read my soul. He wanted me to change my whole way of thinking about myself, at a time when it had never been more important that I hold myself together. And it frightened me how much I craved what he offered; not just sexual ecstasy, but emotional freedom.

"I'm not isolated. You're shadowing my every move, remember?" I hurled it out like an insult, but all I earned from him was an admonishing frown. I turned from him sharply, no longer able to face him. I had been hit with too much in the last few days. And Reed was just making everything worse by forcing me to look at hard truths about myself.

"Where are you going?"

"To take a shower. Are you going to follow me in there, too?" I spat the words as though they were bitter in my mouth. And they were bitter, because a part of me wanted that.

Reed didn't respond, so I continued to stalk the last few steps toward the bathroom and slammed the door behind me. I tried to cling to my anger, but fear burned through it. My fingers were trembling when I struggled to undo my shirt buttons. I suddenly longed to step under the shower's hot spray, to scour my stalker's touch from my skin.

When I stepped under the cascading water, I turned it up as hot as it would go, but my skin still felt cold. The iciness seeped all the way down to my bones, and my teeth chattered.

The shower curtain pulled back, and I let out a little shocked squeak.

"To answer your question," Reed said as he stepped in behind me, "yes, I am going to follow you in here. You won't get rid of me that easily, Katie." His arms closed around me, caging me in. His naked body pressed against mine, and his cock instantly began to harden against my hip.

"I don't want you in here!" I lied and tried to push him away. He held me firmly.

"Yes, you do. You're lying because you're scared about the fact that you want me in here."

"You think you're so smart," I hurled at him. "I was just assaulted. Why on earth would I want a man to touch me right now?"

His features twisted to something fierce, but not out of anger at me. He was enraged by the reminder of my stalker's hands on me. Suddenly, he pressed my back up against the wall, and one of his hands pinned my wrists against the tiles above my head. I couldn't help but be reminded of how my attacker had trapped me.

"No!" I gasped, my panic bleeding out. I jerked against his hold.

"Yes," Reed said, his voice as firm as his grip. "You want this, Katie. And I'm not going to let *him* take it from you. I'm not going to let him take you from me. I won't fucking allow it."

His lips came down on mine, ruthlessly parting them to forestall my protest. As soon as his tongue subdued mine, I felt familiar heat gathering between my legs. The fingers of his free hand slid up my thigh to play through my slick folds, and he groaned at the wetness he found there. It was more than just water. He stroked my clit, and I softened further, melting against him.

Abruptly, he gripped me with his whole hand. Two fingers slid into me while his palm ground against my clit. I let out a little shocked cry at the utterly possessive hold. He tore his lips from mine so that he could pin me with his onyx stare.

"This is mine, Katie. Not his. Your pussy, your body. They belong to me."

I couldn't help shuddering at the word *belong*. It was too close to what my stalker had said. Reed mercilessly stroked his fingers against my g-spot, and my eyes flew wide.

"Tell me, Katie. Tell me you belong to me. Not him."

He rotated his palm against my clit as he crooked his fingers inside me. All my fear was blown away by bliss. Yes, I wanted to belong to Reed. I gave myself to him willingly, and that made all the difference.

"I'm yours, Reed."

He bent and nipped my ear sharply. I moaned and rotated my hips against him in wanton abandon.

"Good. Now address me properly."

"I'm yours, Sir."

His hand left me, but my moment of grief at the loss quickly faded when he kicked my ankles apart, spreading my legs. He paused with his cock head teasing the entrance of my pussy.

"I'm clean," he told me, his voice rough with the strain of holding himself back. "Are you on birth control?"

"Yes! Please fuck me, Sir!" My urging was almost fevered.

His sensual lips curved up in a wicked smile. "You learn quickly. Good girl." Then he thrust up into me. I shrieked out my pleasure/pain. I was still sore from our last coupling, but the burn of him stretching me was delicious. He kept my wrists pinned above me as he stroked into me, and the sensation of being restrained by him made me soften further.

His free hand caressed my bottom. His clever fingers found a little patch of sensitive skin just at the top of my ass, and I cried out and squirmed against him in surprised delight. He laughed against my lips, and his fingers dipped lower, spreading me. I went utterly still when he reached my asshole.

"Has anyone ever touched you here?" His voice was roughened by lust, and he ground his hips against me, stimulating my clit as he moved within me. I relaxed in the wake of the flash of pleasure, and the tip of his finger slipped into me. "Answer me."

"No, Sir," the words were barely audible. Intense embarrassment and perverse arousal warred, feeding off one another until my entire body was on fire.

"Good." He rocked into me, and he pressed deeper when I gave again. I knew that only one finger penetrated me, but I had never felt so thoroughly taken. Reed's tongue claimed my mouth again, and he filled me everywhere. I came completely undone under his onslaught. Only his hold on my body kept me upright as pleasure flooded all my senses, in ways I had never imagined possible.

In the midst of my orgasm, I heard his rough shout. Heat lashed my pussy, and primal chemicals in my brain registered increased ecstasy at the sensation of him coming inside me. His full weight bore down on me as he rode out his pleasure.

"Mine," he murmured against my lips.

"Yours."

# Chapter 11

*"Yours."* My lust-drunken promise of the night before was the first thing I recalled in the morning. I kept my eyes closed, hoping to savor the sweet memory in that blissful place between sleeping and waking. But cruel unease pulled my mind to full lucidity. Images of how I had been restrained by my stalker, how helpless and sick I had felt when he touched me, floated to the surface, mingling with my recollections of bliss under Reed's domineering hands.

What was wrong with me? How could I be disgusted by being rendered completely vulnerable and then come flying apart with pleasure at the same treatment only mere hours later?

*Because with Reed, it's consensual,* I acknowledged. But why did my body consent to it? Why did I burn for him when he held me down and told me I belonged to him? I shouldn't want to *belong* to anyone. I was strong, independent. It was wrong to want to allow a man to make me his possession. No matter how gorgeous and sweet and alluring that man was.

I became aware of Reed's low murmur floating in from the sitting room of his hotel suite. I glanced at the clock. 6:21 AM. A long groan left my chest, and I considered rolling over and going back to sleep. What the hell was he doing awake? And working, by the sound of it.

I sighed. If Reed was working, I should be, too. He had exhausted my body, but I had more important things to do than sleep. Maybe I would have to try some more of that damn coffee. Reed had mentioned one with "caramel undertones." That didn't sound terrible.

Without my realizing it, a lopsided smile broke out on my face. I was quickly becoming infatuated with more than just his body. He had saved Gizmo, for god's sake. And he had bled for it. I came to the realization that I wanted my partner more than I had ever wanted any man. And that didn't scare me as much as it should. My mind told me all the reasons it was wrong – we were coworkers, Frank would disapprove, it was obviously tearing my best friend apart. And then there was the disconcerting fact that I craved the sexual pain he gave me.

But those reasons were only things I knew in my mind; I didn't feel them in my heart.

Falling into familiar habits, I moved into action to quiet my busy thoughts. Reed wouldn't approve, but what he didn't know would hurt him. Or hurt me, rather. I knew I would be in trouble with him if he did realize what I was doing.

I shook my head and slipped into one of the fluffy robes provided by the hotel before joining Reed in the next room. He was sitting on the small couch, his shoulders slumped and his brow furrowed. Underneath his natural tan, he appeared pale.

"What's going on?"

His head snapped up, and he ran a hand over his face as though to smooth away the worry he had shown. Within moments, his expression had gone from one of deepest concern to caution. He scooted over and patted the couch beside him.

"Come sit with me, Katie."

"Why?" I asked warily, but I was already walking toward him. My knees folded, and his hand immediately found mine when I sat.

Reed sucked in a long breath and then blew it out slowly. The creases around his eyes betrayed his concern. He appeared deeply shaken, and that scared me more than anything.

"Tell me what's happening. Please." I couldn't bear his tense silence for one more second.

"The results on the contents of the syringe came back." His voice was uncharacteristically quiet, but smooth, almost as though he was trying to soothe me. My dread ratcheted up a notch. "It was Acepromazine Maleate, the same animal tranquilizer that we

found in Martel's house. The one he used to subdue his victims."
My breath caught in my throat as I came to the horrifying
conclusion Reed was about to utter. "Your attacker said he was
leaving you a clue about how to find him. Katie, I think your
stalker is The Mentor."

*Maybe not,* my mind denied desperately. Maybe there was
some sort of common brand used by the most heinous criminals.
Maybe they all shopped at the same store. Creepers-R-Us. My
stalker could be some other sadistic man who abducted and
tortured women.

But deep down, I knew that wasn't true. Part of me had
always known, or at least had always suspected. I just didn't want
to acknowledge it. Somehow, it had been easier to deal with when
it was some amateur psycho. It wasn't just Parnell trying to scare
me, like Reed had suggested. Now I knew my stalker was a coolly
calculating master criminal who took special pleasure in sexual
torture.

*It's just a case. He's a case, like all the others. Think.
This is what I do. This is my job.* I was good at this. If I could
stop back and think objectively, the crippling terror might go away.

"What else did we find? Is there anything on the blindfold?
What about cameras in the hotel? And what about the prints on the
notes he sent me?"

Reed looked at me queerly, as though he knew I was barely
clinging on to sanity. He was right, but I couldn't think about that.
If I did, I would be sick. I would curl into a ball and cry and let
Reed protect me and take care of everything. That wasn't an
option.

"The only DNA hits on the blindfold were your hair and
skin cells. Forensics is going to trace the cloth fibers and see if
they can figure out the material's origins. The camera feed in the
hotel was down for half an hour around the time you were
attacked. There weren't any prints on the syringe other than mine,
and the notes only came up with prints of people in the unit; you,

Dex, and Frank. We knew they would show up." He ran a frustrated hand through his hair. "We should have been more careful with the evidence. Everyone is letting their concern for you cloud their judgment."

I nodded my agreement, relived that Reed was insistent on making this less personal. "Yes. We need to treat this like any other case. In a way, this is almost better. It gives us more information about The Mentor's mindset, and it ties my stalker to the investigative process we've already begun."

"Nothing about this is good, Katie." Reed almost snapped at me.

My eyes narrowed, warning him not to push me. "Some good will come of this, Reed. Based on my attacker's behavior, we know The Mentor is familiar with investigative techniques. And we know he has a certain weakness when it comes to me. The more he toys with me, the more we find out about his mindset and methods. He's arrogant. That arrogance might cause him to overplay his hand." My voice lowered, softening. "This is how I have to deal with this, Reed. Please."

His grip on my hand eased, going from crushing to comforting. "Okay, Katie," he allowed. "Our next step is to track down Parnell. We left him to Colton because I wanted to keep you away from this, but now it's our job. Catching The Mentor is our assignment, and if he's a threat to you, I want to put all my resources into bringing him down. And you're right," he said grudgingly. "You're his weakness. He wants you to find him, so we'll fucking find him. Together." The last word was heavy with significance. *Trust me,* his hard black eyes demanded.

"Together," I agreed.

∎∎∎∎∎∎∎∎∎∎∎∎∎∎∎∎∎∎∎∎∎∎∎∎∎∎∎∎∎∎∎∎∎∎∎∎∎∎∎∎∎∎∎∎∎∎∎∎∎∎∎∎

"We suspect Parnell's girlfriend is either sheltering him or at least knows where he's hiding out. Somehow, the little weasel knows we're looking for him, and he's gone to ground. I'll never understand how sick fucks like this trick women into loving them." Colton's lips were curled in distaste as he shoved Parnell's file across the desk for my examination.

"It's camouflage," I remarked as I flipped it open. "Parnell can be very charismatic. Having a girlfriend makes him blend in with normal people."

I was familiar with the file's contents, but I couldn't help staring at the dishwater brown eyes that looked up at me from his photograph. If it weren't for his eyes, he might have been attractive. He was fifty-five years old, but his angular face was only lightly lined, and streaks of dark blond persisted in his greying hair. Most women would consider him a silver fox. Unfortunately for the women he had raped and killed, they hadn't seen the monster behind the beautiful exterior before it was too late.

"As much as I want to see him behind bars, I really don't think Parnell is The Mentor." I had already told Reed, but I felt the need to share my doubts with Colton. "The Mentor's notes to me indicate that he cares about being with me in some sick way. Parnell has made lewd comments, but he doesn't keep the women he abducts. And he doesn't drug them. He seduces them to get them alone, rapes them, and kills them. He doesn't hold them for long periods of time and use them up like Martel did. It makes more sense if The Mentor shares Martel's M.O." Two years of practice helped me keep my voice neutral. "Parnell isn't smart enough to be The Mentor. He went through too many women, too fast. That's how we found him. Based on Lydia Chase's testimony, The Mentor encouraged Martel to keep his victims alive for as long as possible in order to avoid being caught." I pressed my lips together, unable to say more and keep my cool façade.

Colton got that pigheaded look I knew all too well. "Parnell is our best lead. He has a known history of violence toward women, and he hunts in the Chicago area. I'm bringing him in for questioning."

"If it isn't Parnell, at least we can rule him out," Reed supplied before I could further argue my point.

"Okay," I allowed. "Maybe we can get some new charges to stick in the other cases if we question him again." I still couldn't believe that the CPD had lost the evidence we needed to convict him. "Do you think you can get to him through the girlfriend?" I asked Colton.

"If she won't talk, I'll put a tail on her. We'll find Parnell, Katie." He said it as though that was going to put an end to the investigation. He really believed Parnell was the man stalking me. I didn't want to waste my time trying to convince him otherwise. Reed was right. Questioning Parnell would allow us to rule him out, at the very least, and maybe we would be able to gather more evidence for a conviction.

"In the meantime," I turned my focus on Reed, "I think we should go through missing person cases involving women in the Chicago area. We'll go back decades if we need to. The Mentor is at least Martel's age, likely older, so that puts him in his late thirties at the youngest. He knows what he's doing, so – judging by the fact that he keeps his victims for prolonged periods – we know he probably has years of experience. It'll be a lot of work, but if we locate women who were found alive after experiencing sexual assault, we can bring them in for questioning. It might be that one of them got away from The Mentor." Even as I said the words, I doubted them. The Mentor was too smart and neat to allow a woman to escape him. But Lydia Chase had gotten away from his student Carl Martel, so I wasn't going to rule out the possibility. The Mentor had to have started somewhere. Maybe he was sloppier when he was younger.

"Good idea," Reed said. "We should get back to the field office and get started. Do you think Dex will give us a hand?"

I flinched at Dex's name. I was trying to ignore what had happened between us in the elevator. *"I fucking love you, Katie."* So much had happened since then that it hadn't been as hard as it should have been to push it away. Now it pounded at the edges of my thoughts, demanding to be acknowledged.

"No," I said, my voice tight. "He's still busy with the client list from Dusk. You and I should handle this until we have some solid leads." My gaze found Colton's again. "Keep me updated on Parnell."

"Will do. We'll bring him in soon, Katie." Again, I got the sense that he was certain Parnell was The Mentor. I resisted the urge to shake my head. I knew deep in my bones that he was wrong. Parnell could never devise the horrors The Mentor indulged in. He was greedy and didn't think beyond the quick kill, the little burst of pleasure he found in tormenting women. The Mentor savored them.

I couldn't suppress a shudder. Reed's hand gripped my elbow in a show of support. I realized all the blood had drained from my face.

*It's just another case. It's just another case.* The reassurance was hollow, because all my cases haunted me. *I hate my job.*

• • • • • • • • • • • • • • • • • • • • • • • • • • • • • • • • • • • • • • • • • • • • • • • • • • • • • • • • •

By the time Reed and I entered his hotel room late that night, I was exhausted and sickened. Spending a day pouring over sexual assault cases will do that to a person. We had spent hours going through missing person cases, and we had barely scratched the surface. The number of women who had been found alive was far too small. The cold cases and murders, on the other hand, were available in abundance.

Reed looked just as weary as I felt. Days like today sucked. Really, all of my days sucked. I wasn't sure how much longer I could keep this up without crumbling.

Without warning, his arms closed around me, and he pulled my body up against his chest. I almost protested that I didn't need a hug, but that would be a lie, and Reed didn't tolerate lies. Besides, there was a desperate tautness to his muscles that let me know I wasn't the only one who needed to be held. The show of vulnerability was shocking. I let out a shaky laugh to cover the depth of my emotion.

"I didn't think big bad Doms needed hugs," I teased weakly.

He gave me a wan smile. "I'm still human, Katie. I need my sub's strength just as much as she needs mine."

*My sub.* My heart fluttered at the sound of that even as my gut clenched.

In the space of a second, his tired eyes turned reproving. "Don't do that," he ordered. "Don't hide from me."

"I'm right here," I evaded the truth.

He tapped the center of my forehead with a long finger. "Don't hide from me, Katie."

I pursed my lips and looked away so that he couldn't look into my soul. But he had no mercy for me. He sensed my weakness in my exhaustion, and he took advantage. I let out a little surprised squeak when the world tilted around me, and I found myself cradled in his arms. He settled down on the couch, keeping me in his lap with his arms wrapped around my waist and shoulders, pinning my arms in. My head seemed to find the crook between his chin and chest of its own accord, and I breathed out a long sigh. Being held by him like this felt undeniably good.

"Talk to me," it was a low command. "Why do you feel like you have to hide your emotions from me? Why are you afraid to be vulnerable? You should never be afraid of me, Katie."

I peered up into his gorgeous face, taking in the open earnestness of his perfect features. "I'm not afraid of you. I'm afraid of failure. I'm afraid of being a disappointment." I caught my lower lip between my teeth, worried I had confessed too much.

"Who are you afraid to disappoint?"

I hesitated. "Frank," I admitted softly. "He took me in after my father died. He's..." I fumbled. "Well, you've met him. He's a very hard man. With a strong sense of right and wrong. He's completely devoted to his job. But he can be different around me. Sometimes, he's gentle. He was my father's partner, and he held me when I cried after he was killed. I was so in awe of how he was able to pull his life together and devote himself to his work, to a higher cause. I felt I needed to do the same. If I followed his example, I would be able to go on without my father, too."

"Did Frank tell you to join the FBI?" Reed quietly prompted me to keep talking, to keep spilling my deepest secrets. Now that I had started, I couldn't seem to stop. It felt too good.

"He kind of guided me to it, made sure I was accepted to Quantico and got a good position working for him. But he never told me I had to do it."

"If you told him you're unhappy with your job, do you think he would tell you to stay?"

"I..." I had never thought about it like that before. "I don't know. He's proud of the work I do. I can't imagine doing anything else."

"Can't you?"

The two words were the final blow to my walls, and I revealed my deepest-held secret. "Before my father died, I wanted to study to be a vet. I hate my job."

"I know you do." He paused. "I didn't know your father, Katie, but do you think he would want you to be unhappy?"

"No," the word came out on a soft sob. My tears wet Reed's shirt, and he traced reassuring patterns on my upper arm with his thumb.  The gesture was soothing, hypnotic.  My tears stopped flowing when I fell asleep in his arms.

# Chapter 12

"You don't have to go in there, Katie," Colton told me, his voice gentle.

Claude Parnell stared through the one-way mirror in the CPD interrogation room. Rationally, I knew he couldn't possibly be looking at me; there was no way he could see me through the glass. But the smirk on his face and the mocking light in his eyes was the same as I remembered. This wasn't a man who was afraid of me, despite my position.

"Agent Byrd," he called in a singsong voice. "I know you're out there. Come in and play."

I did my best to pretend I hadn't heard him. "Where did you find him?" I asked Colton.

"The girlfriend's house. We managed to go in with probable cause, but it'll be hard to justify once his lawyer gets here. I was a little, um, aggressive about getting in. If we don't get him to say something incriminating, he'll walk out of here in a few hours."

My resolve hardened. Even though I didn't believe Parnell was The Mentor, I wasn't going to let him get away again. He would hurt more women, and he would know to be more careful now. I wasn't going to let that happen.

"I'm going in," I declared.

Reed's hand closed around my arm, stopping me short. "Katie. Are you sure that's a good idea?"

"Yes. He's a sick bastard, but that'll work to my advantage. He won't talk to you guys, but he might slip up if he's taunting me."

*I hate my job.* The hard press of Reed's lips let me know he had read my thoughts, and he didn't approve of my decision. I had revealed too much in his arms the night before. I couldn't do my job properly if Reed's understanding dark eyes kept tempting me to break down and let him handle everything for me. The prospect of allowing him to protect me was too tempting for me to contemplate. I had to protect myself, or I would never make it out of this alive. Or worse, I would find myself alive and in the hands of The Mentor.

I suppressed a shudder. *Parnell isn't The Mentor,* I reminded myself. He couldn't be. It didn't fit with his M.O. And it was too easy to pin it on him. If anything, The Mentor hoped we would arrest Parnell for his crimes. He would make an ideal scapegoat.

"I need to do this, Reed." I pointedly extricated myself from his grip.

"I don't like it," Colton crossed his arms over his chest. "Last time-"

"Last time, I let him get to me. That won't happen again." *Because I've faced worse since then, and Parnell isn't The Mentor.*

I took a deep breath and schooled my features to a professional blank before stepping into the interrogation room. Parnell's eyes found mine instantly, and a slow smile bared his teeth. His gazed raked down my body in a leisurely progression from my face down my legs and back again, lingering on my sex and breasts.

*He's not The Mentor. He's not The Mentor.* If I told myself enough times, I might just remember it. The reassurance threatened to fly out of my head as Parnell's dirty dishwater eyes settled on mine again. My stomach churned as my primal mind recognized a predator. I had been conditioned to fight, but my nature was inclined towards flight.

Calling on my training, I consciously chose fight. I lifted my chin and sat in the metal chair across the table from Parnell. It was far too narrow. I could smell the tobacco on his breath, could see every dark hair in his five-o-clock shadow. The fine lines around his eyes deepened with his leer, revealing the monster that hid behind the handsome mask.

"It's been a while, Katherine," his voice was low and sensual, almost melodic.

"It's Agent Byrd," I corrected him coldly. "Where were you Wednesday between the hours of seven and eight PM?" *During the time when I was assaulted.*

His grin widened. "I like a strong woman, *Agent Byrd.* They're so much more fun to break."

"Where were you Wednesday between the hours of seven and eight PM?" I repeated in a monotone. I couldn't allow him to divert me from my purpose.

"Determined," he remarked. "I like that, too. The determined ones always fight harder."

"So you enjoy raping women." I tried to catch him out.

His smile was condescending. "Did I say that? I don't believe I did."

"Wednesday," I prompted. "Between seven and eight PM. Where were you?"

"With Jolene. But you already knew that."

"I don't know that," I corrected him. "I know CPD officers found you hiding out at her house this morning. Hiding behind a woman like a little bitch."

I expected a snarl or an outburst. I hoped to provoke him. But he just laughed. "Jolene's useful. I was with her for the last two weeks. You can ask her."

"And I'm sure she'll back you up. That is, until we arrest her for aiding and abetting. How long do you think she'll protect you then?" I placed special emphasis on *protect* in an effort to shame him. A man like Parnell reveled in power over women, and the suggestion that he was reliant on one in any way should piss him off. It should make him sloppy.

"You can't arrest her for that," he called my bluff. "Who is she *aiding and abetting*? I'm not a criminal. I've never been convicted of anything, and you don't seem to be charging me with anything, either."

"I'll do whatever I have to to get her to talk," I assured him. "I'll find out if you're lying."

He shrugged. "You want to know where I was between seven and eight PM on Wednesday? I was fucking her. I was fucking her, but I wasn't *with* her. You see, I was thinking about you, Katherine. Jolene's a kinky bitch. She lets me choke her while I fuck her. I was thinking about how my hands would look around your throat. You have such beautiful skin. I bet it would turn a nice shade of red while I choked you. You're a kinky bitch, too, aren't you, Kathy?"

*Kathy.* Fear curled up my throat, cutting off my air as effectively as Parnell's hands.

"Oh, look. Now you've gone all pale. Very pretty skin. So expressive."

"You're threatening to murder a Federal Agent," I forced out.

His sick smile stayed fixed firmly in place. "I didn't say anything about killing you. I wouldn't kick a woman like you out of bed that quickly."

An insinuation that he would want to keep a victim around for a while. And he called me Kathy.

*He's not The Mentor. He's not The Mentor.*

Wasn't he? When The Mentor had attacked me, I couldn't read anything about his identity. Was he sitting right across from me, taunting me?

No. It couldn't be. It didn't make any sense.

"I didn't think you liked to keep your women for long before you raped and murdered them," I remarked as calmly as I could manage.

"Aren't you a cold one? Throwing out words like *rape* and *murder* like it doesn't bother you. But I know it does, Kathy.

Underneath that ice, you burn hot. I could break that ice. You'd be such a hot fuck. You need to be broken."

I wanted to vomit, I wanted to run, but he was getting so close to confessing something he shouldn't. And so close to telling me whether or not he really was The Mentor.

*"You'll come to love me,"* he had said.

"So you think breaking me will make me love you? Is that what you want? Love?" I did my best impression of a scoff. "I didn't think you were that much of a pussy, Parnell."

He jerked against the handcuffs that secured him to the table and growled at me. I had finally gotten to him. "I don't want your fucking *love*, bitch. I want your cunt. I want your screams. I want to watch the light leave your eyes. I want me fucking you raw to be the last thing you know."

I knew I should feel triumph. The threat was enough for us to hold him for a little while. Maybe we could get some charges to stick. But all I felt was soul-deep disgust.

He leaned toward me, and his putrid breath fanned across my face. "You think you know me. You don't know shit. We'll get better acquainted soon."

The door opened behind me, and righteous rage pulsed into the room. A familiar hand came down on my shoulder in a protective gesture, and I looked up to find Frank standing at my side. His hard eyes were fixed on Parnell.

"You won't be getting anywhere near her." He spoke calmly, quietly. It was more terrifying than if he had shouted. "You're going to rot in prison. You'll die there, if I have any say in it. And I do."

Parnell paled as he realized his mistake. He had provoked my dad, and now the full power of the FBI was going to come down on him. He looked like he might piss himself.

Frank gave my shoulder a little squeeze. "Come on, Katie." He walked me out of the room, and I found solace in his strength at my side. Surely he could see that my job was tearing me apart. He wouldn't want that for me. Maybe it was time to talk to him about a career change.

To my surprise, he didn't let me go once we were outside interrogation. Instead, his arm wrapped around my shoulders, and he pulled me close. He rarely touched me in front of other people like this. It went against his hard-ass persona. He must be really worried about me to make such an aggressive show of support. That almost scared me more than anything, even as I found comfort in his protection.

I noticed Colton shift uncomfortably on his feet, and I realized that Frank was staring him down.

"What do you think you're doing, sending her in there with Parnell?" He asked the captain in that same low, dangerous voice.

It was Reed who answered. "It was Katie's decision. We respected that." He wasn't throwing me under the bus; he was supporting me, like a partner should.

It wasn't a smart move. Frank's glare turned on Reed, and I almost stepped between them to shield Reed from its piercing force. But he didn't need my help. He swallowed, but he met Frank squarely in the eye. After what felt like an eternity, Frank gave him a short nod of acknowledgement. I could hardly believe it.

Then his stare turned on me. I would have stepped away if it weren't for his arm around my shoulders holding me in place.

"Don't do anything like that again," he reprimanded. "I know you're a great agent, but you don't have to handle things like this on your own."

I marveled at the words. I had never expected Frank to tell me it was okay to lean on someone else. Reed might be right, after all. Frank just wanted what was best for me. And if what was best for me didn't include working for the FBI, he just might approve.

As soon as I caught The Mentor, I was going to talk to him about my career path. Animals were so much kinder than humans.

Despite everything that was happening, I felt as though a weight had been lifted from my shoulders.

■■■■■■■■■■■■■■■■■■■■■■■■■■■■■■■■■■■■■■■■■■■■■■■■■■■■■

"Do I want the good news or the bad news first?" Reed asked his friend with the easy humor of familiarity, but there was a tense undercurrent to his tone. Smith James' expression was a twisted mask of anger. The senior agent from the New York field office had flown to Chicago under the pretense of visiting his fiancé's family, but now he was sitting in Reed's hotel suite, grim-faced.

"The good news is the bad news." His voice was deep and gravelly, but not from weariness. I had met Smith a few times before, and I knew this was just his usual ferocity, turned up a few notches. "You remember the Latin King, Hugo Reyes, who we arrested when we busted Decadence for drug trafficking?"

Reed gave a tight, satisfied nod. "The fucker I put in a coma. I remember him."

"Well, he's awake now, and not so brain damaged that he's forgotten what you did to him and why. He's turned on the Kings in exchange for being sent to a minimum security prison. He feels safer with the white collar criminals than his brothers in the gang. His brush with death has brought him to the realization that he doesn't want to die for them, after all."

"If you're talking to us, I'm guessing his information pertains to more than just the Kings in New York," I surmised. "But why are we meeting here and not at the field office?"

He eyed me carefully, assessing. I shifted under his scrutiny, and his features eased to something more genial. "Because I trust Reed, and he trusts you."

"So what did Reyes have to say that's so important you couldn't tell us over the phone or through email?" Reed prompted.

"You remember how the Kings knew to try to run just before we came in for the bust? We managed to round them up anyway, but the Russians got away," his lips thinned. "Reyes said they were tipped off. He identified the man who warned him as Carl Martel. So now we know how Martel knew to get out before we came in. He abandoned Lydia to save his own skin. The chaos that ensued when the Kings tried to escape gave him the opportunity to slip past us."

"But who told Martel to get out?" I came to the same nauseating conclusion he obviously had. "His only ally. The Mentor. And the only way The Mentor would have known we were coming is if-"

"He's one of us," Reed finished for me. "He's NYPD or FBI."

"It makes sense," Smith rumbled. "Martel was always one step ahead of us. He knew when and where he could get to Lydia without getting caught." He paused and closed his eyes briefly, clearly reining in his fury at the memories of what had been done to the woman he loved; Lydia Chase was his fiancé. "Then there's the sniper attack on Tucker Chase and the advanced tech Martel used, but there isn't any evidence of him having those skill sets."

I paled, remembering the video clip of Reed and me that had appeared on my computer. That hadn't been the work of an amateur stalker; it had been The Mentor. "Have we gotten anything off my computer?" I asked Reed. "You know, after…" I trailed off, hoping no one had been able to recover the video even as I knew we needed more clues.

"Completely fried," Reed responded, his hand finding mine. "Tech couldn't salvage anything."

I forced myself to remain in professional mode. "But what's the link between Martel and The Mentor? Why would The Mentor go to such lengths for him?"

*"You're very brave. That makes me… happy."* I remembered the words he had spoken to me as he held me down, his cock hardening against me.

"The Mentor is insane. He admitted it when he…" I swallowed. "When I was with him. He seemed almost surprised that he felt any emotion for me at all. My guess is he's a psychopath. What bond did he share with Martel to make him care enough to protect his mentee?" I turned back to the only lead we had. "What about the list of patrons at Dusk? There was one who's FBI, and he's in the New York field-"

"No!" Smith barked, and I shrank back. "Don't you dare say Kennedy's name. I owe him everything that I am. He's a good man."

"My name and Dex's are on the list, too," Reed reminded me, effectively cutting off what was sure to be a tirade from Smith. The man was intimidating, and I had inched toward Reed for support without realizing it. Smith's eyes fell on my white-knuckled grip on my partner's hand, and he backed off.

"You don't know him, but I do. So does Reed. Kennedy could never do something like this." Smith's voice was gentler this time, and some of the tension left me. I hadn't at all enjoyed being caught in his furor.

"All right, then," my voice barely trembled. "The client list at Dusk has gotten us nowhere, we can't find anything about Martel's family other than his murdered parents, and now we know that Parnell's probably not The Mentor." What started out as a confident list of facts turned defeated by the end. What more did we have?

"We're still going through the missing person cases," Reed reminded me. "We might find something there. And now we know he's in law enforcement. That'll help narrow our search. We're not back at square one, Katie," he reassured me.

I was almost terrified to ask, but it was the only other next step I could think of. "What about Lydia?" I didn't look Smith in the eye. "Could I talk to her again? If she remembers anything-"

Smith let out a warning growl, and my teeth snapped closed.

"I think it's Lydia's choice." Reed fixed Smith with a significant stare.

After a long, tense silence, Smith snapped, "Fine. You're right. It's her choice. I just want to keep her safe, but I have to remember that she doesn't like it when I make decisions for her," he said the last with fondness, and I was relieved at his renewed warmth. Lydia obviously brought out his softer side as well as triggering his ferocity when it came to defending her. "I'll ask her tonight. I know it's important to her that The Mentor is caught. She worries constantly about the women he might be hurting." He turned kind silver eyes on me. "And I know she likes you, Agent Byrd. If she'll talk to anyone, it'll be you."

"Thanks," I said, slightly abashed. I had been the first agent Lydia had opened up to after she had been found at Decadence, after Martel had abandoned her. She had been so destroyed inside. That conversation still haunted me. It wasn't something I looked forward to repeating, but if she was strong enough to talk about it, I would have to be strong enough to listen.

"Okay," Smith stood. "I have to get back to her. I don't like her being in Chicago and out of my sight." His eyes glowed as he looked from Reed to me, impressing his will upon us. "This conversation doesn't leave this room. I don't trust anyone else. Except Clayton and Kennedy," his gaze burned into me as he spoke his boss' name.

My heart squeezed. I shared the same faith in Dex and Frank, but I didn't dare tell Smith that I would utter a word to either of them.

I thought about Colton. Didn't I trust him, too? He had been so sure Parnell was The Mentor. And I knew Parnell would have made the perfect scapegoat. He had weaseled his way out of being imprisoned for his known crimes because the CPD had lost the evidence against him.

*Someone in law enforcement.*

I recalled my blindness when The Mentor had assaulted me, how he had masked every aspect of his identity. He had been so close that he had touched me, and I was still no closer to learning who he was.

*I can't trust anyone.*

# Chapter 13

It was still so strange lounging in bed next to Reed, as though it was the most natural thing in the world. Passion had lead me here on other nights, and exhaustion the night before. But now we had both showered and brushed our teeth and gotten into bed, as though we were a normal couple going about our usual routines.

Thankfully, Reed had brought a variety of clothes from my apartment, so I wasn't stuck with just pajamas. I had a sneaking suspicion he had included the silky green nightgown with white lace on purpose, but I didn't mind. It was far less embarrassing than my animal print PJs. The only thing embarrassing about this was the fact that my hard nipples were clearly visible against the thin material. That was something Reed didn't seem to mind.

He also didn't seem to mind sleeping in nothing but boxers.

"Don't you have a t-shirt or something?" I asked. The intensity of my attraction to him still scared me somewhat, and having him mostly naked wasn't helping.

He laughed at me. "Well, aren't you prudish all of a sudden? You didn't mind looking at my cock in the shower. Besides, the boxers are a courtesy. I usually don't wear anything to bed." The playful sparkle in his eyes faded. "I thought you might appreciate some space between us tonight. I understand if you want me to sleep on the couch."

"What? Why?"

"After everything that's happened with The Mentor, and today with Parnell, I figured you might not want to be near a man." The words seemed to pain him, as though it went against his nature to put distance between us. I remembered how he had touched me so boldly in the shower, burning away memories of my stalker's touch. He obviously wanted to do the same again, to claim me after the vile things Parnell had said about raping me, but he also seemed to sense that I had hit some kind of breaking point.

A part of me thought he was right. But at the same time, I couldn't bear the thought of his distance. I needed Reed's strength beside me, despite my fears about what needing him said about me. I was coming to accept that I didn't have to be strong and independent all the time, that it was okay to show vulnerability. But I couldn't afford to think like that just yet. I had to catch The Mentor before I could think about changing my life.

"I don't want you to go," I said quietly. "Today was horrible, but something good came of it. The way Frank was so protective of me… It made me realize he wants me to be safe and happy." I took a deep breath, ready to make the admission out loud. "I think you might be right, Reed. Frank would have never wanted me to join the FBI if he realized how much I hate it."

His eyes widened. "You're really thinking about quitting?"

I bit my lip. "I think so," I whispered, as though I was afraid to say the words. "But not yet. I have to catch The Mentor first. And I'm worried…" I hesitated. "I'm worried when I stop being strong, all my grief about my dad will come back and I'll have to go through mourning all over again. I don't know if I can handle that, Reed. I'm… I'm scared."

"Come here," his voice was soft as he wrapped an arm around my waist and scooted my body closer to his. I rested my head on his shoulder, taking comfort in his steady warmth. "If you do have to grieve, I'll be right here with you."

"You lost your mother," I remembered. "How do you deal with it? With her being gone?"

"Losing her shaped my whole life. I wouldn't be who I am if things had happened differently. And I know she'd be proud of who I've become. I miss her, but I can't change the past. All I can do is choose how to live now."

"You said you were fourteen when she died. How did it happen?" I knew the question was intensely personal, but Reed had never been anything but unflinchingly honest and open with me. And I had shared some of my deepest secrets with him.

"She was stabbed to death." He paused, as though it took effort to say the next words. "By my father."

"Oh my god, Reed. I'm so sorry." The words weren't enough, but what else could I say? The prospect was horrific. How was Reed able to live with what had happened to her?

"I am, too. She didn't deserve that." His eyes met mine, and I saw a wealth of sadness in them. His hand twined in my hair, working through the coppery strands with a tenderness that shocked me. "She had a gentle heart, like you. But she wasn't as strong, and she was impulsive. She married my father after knowing him for a month, before she had the chance to realize what he was. Cristian Sánchez was a Colombian drug lord. He was at his home in Atlanta at the time when she met him. My father was very charismatic, and he was never cruel to her. I believe he truly loved her."

My lips parted, and I hung on to every word. Reed's father was a drug lord? And now Reed was FBI? How did that work? I kept my silence, waiting for him to tell me the rest.

"My mother loved him, too, even though she hated the violence in his life. She didn't want me to have any part of it. She kept me in Atlanta with her when my father would travel for his business. She even named me for her father instead of naming me after Cristian, like he wanted. But when I was fourteen, my father decided I was old enough to start learning the family business. My mother had tried so hard to keep me away from it. She tried to run with me. My father went into a fit of rage, and he stabbed her for trying to leave him. He grieved after, as though he hadn't been the one to do it." Reed's lips twisted in disgust.

"I managed to get away," he continued. "I went to my mother's parents, and my father didn't dare follow me there. He knew I could report him for killing my mother, so we had a tacit understanding not to threaten each other. I even took my grandparents' surname – Miller – to further distance myself from my father.

"When I graduated college, I joined the Atlanta Police Department. I had only served for a year when they asked me to help them go after my father. I still hated him for what he had done to my mother, so I agreed. I went in on the raid with the APD. My father pulled a gun on me and shot me in the chest. I would have died if it hadn't been for the Kevlar. My partner shot him to protect me. I watched Cristian die. And I felt nothing but satisfaction."

He turned a worried gaze on me, as though concerned he had said too much.

"He killed your mother," I said, letting him know that I understood. Reed had never loved his father, and Cristian had taken his one real parent from him. There were times I wished the man who had shot my father was dead. There were times I dreamed about killing him myself. My mother died giving birth to me, and Daddy had been my everything.

Reed nodded, his eyes clearing with relief that I hadn't judged him. "As soon as I turned twenty-four and was eligible for the FBI, I applied to be a Special Agent. I was accepted at Quantico because of the work I did to bring my father down."

His thumb traced the line of my cheekbone. "I felt so powerless in the years after my mother's death," he confessed. "When I was eighteen, I found BDSM. It helped me channel my emotions. It helped me understand myself and take control. I wouldn't be who I am without it." He brushed a kiss across my lips. "I know you're still scared of it, and I understand why. With the things you see at work every day, I know why your desires confuse you. But you don't have to be afraid of them, Katie. I would never do anything to hurt you. You know that, right?"

The tension in his muscles let me know how important my answer was to him. "Yes," I breathed. "I know you wouldn't hurt me, Reed. Not really. But you're right. I am scared. I'm scared of what you make me feel. I'm scared to change how I live my life. I don't know how to be any other way."

His forefinger curled beneath my chin. "Then let me show you."

I stayed completely still as he slowly leaned into me. His satisfied smirk let me know he enjoyed trapping me with nothing more than his power over me. And I *was* powerless when it came to him. I was powerless, and I loved every heady second of my helplessness to resist him.

When his lips came down on mine, it was like coming home; sweetest joy and the deep satisfaction found in familiarity. His mouth slanted over mine, the nip of his teeth urging me to open for him. I complied, sighing into him, reveling in the comfort and ecstasy of his kiss. Our connection was electric; our bodies recognized the natural bond shared by our souls, even if we didn't fully realize it yet. Reed was my perfect fit in every way, physically and emotionally. The rush of feelings for him brought my fear creeping back up through my bliss. It was too much, too fast.

I tried to pull away, but Reed only barely allowed my lips to break from his. He cradled the back of my head, blocking my retreat.

"I won't hurt you, remember?" His voice was as smooth as dark velvet. "You don't have to be afraid with me."

"I'm not afraid that you'll hurt me. I'm scared of what I feel for you."

Lines of concern appeared around his eyes, but he didn't release me. "Why?"

"We're partners, Reed," I evaded the real reason. "We shouldn't be doing this."

"No," he agreed. "We shouldn't. But that's not going to stop me." His mouth took mine with a low growl, and I was lost. He felt too good to fight.

His lips left mine to trace the line of my jaw and plant soft kisses on the column of my neck. He paused at the hollow beneath my ear and blew a stream of cool air across the sensitive area. I shivered, my skin pebbling in delight. Then his teeth closed around my lobe. I gasped and arched into him as the little flare pain caused an answering tug between my legs. His tongue traced the shell of my ear, and the sensation heightened my growing lust. I had never known this area of my body could be so erotic, but Reed knew just how to manipulate me.

"I'm going to explore you tonight," he whispered across my sensitized flesh, and I shuddered in delight. "I don't want you to be scared. Just be a good girl and accept the pleasure I give you. I promise you won't regret it." His teeth nipped my ear again, tugging, and I moaned. That low, cocky chuckle I loved so much only got me hotter for him.

His lips returned to mine, and his hold on the back of my neck remained firm as his body weight gently pressed me down against the mattress. His hands skimmed up the length of my arms, stretching them above me in a wide V. I heard a faint tinkling, and then something was closing around my right wrist. I jerked my mouth from his and craned my neck to see what he was doing. His body held mine down as he finished securing the black leather cuff around my wrist. I was so entranced by the sight of it that he had time to ensnare my other wrist before I started struggling.

"What is this, Reed?" I demanded, but my voice was strangely breathy. I knew I should be panicking; The Mentor had warned me that he would keep me restrained. But I was lost in the moment with Reed. I trusted him. And that arrogant grin of his made me melt.

"Under the bed restraints," he explained as though it was completely obvious. He scooted down my body, and within seconds my ankles were cuffed.

"When did you install these?" I knew the hotel didn't come with them attached to the bed, and it struck me that Reed must have planned this in advance.

He shrugged. "When I first brought your stuff in from your apartment. I set up a few surprises." His smile turned wicked. "After that first kiss, I knew I had to have you like this. I went slowly with you; I'm still going slowly with you. But it'll be worth it." His hands fisted in the front of my nightgown. "It's a shame to ruin this."

"What?"

The fabric gave with one jerk of his arms, the delicate material splitting down the middle, leaving me exposed. He reached over into the bedside drawer and pulled out something that was a garish, sparkly purple.

Oh, god. *My vibrator.* The little rabbit that had been my friend now seemed to smirk at me. My entire body flushed crimson.

His eyes danced with his amusement. "This is a very pretty toy you have here. I'll make you show me how you use it sometime. But for tonight, I'm pretty sure I can figure out how it works."

"Reed, you can't-" My protest died in my throat when he placed two fingers across my lips, silencing me.

"I can, and I will. Your only way out of this is a safe word." He flicked the vibrator on and placed it on the bed just between my legs, so close that I could feel the sheets move with its vibrations, but it didn't quite touch my flesh.

Mortification and desire warred within me, and a low, animal whine eased up from my chest.

"I found something else interesting in your apartment," Reed informed me. "The contents of your ereader were very entertaining."

I tugged against my restraints as a fresh wave of embarrassment washed over me. He had found my collection of BDSM romance novels. "That's private!"

His eyes were unrepentant. "Then you should have put a locking passcode on it. Besides," his face was suddenly inches from mine, and his hand closed around my pussy in a possessive grip, "nothing of yours is private from me. Your whole body is open for me now. And I'm going to sample and explore and own every inch of you."

A little whimper fluttered in the back of my throat at his crass words, and his teeth flashed brilliant white.

"You want that, don't you, Katie?" He asked for an answer he already knew. But he wanted to force me to admit it, to accept what he was doing to me. I nodded, but it wasn't enough for him. "Say it. Tell me you want this."

"I want this, Sir," my voice trembled slightly. "I want you, Reed."

He kissed me in reward, slow and deep. Breathtaking. My head was spinning by the time he released me, and my body ached for stimulation. The light vibrations of my rabbit teased along my inner thighs, but I needed more.

Reed retrieved another item from the drawer, and my eyes widened. The black strip of cloth sent a spike of fear through my system. He was with me instantly, his hand stroking my hair in a soothing rhythm.

"I know why this frightens you, Katie," he told me in a low, even voice. "But I don't want it to. I don't want *him* to take it from you. You trusted me before. Trust me again."

I remembered how he had held my arms above my head in the shower, how I had flashbacks to my stalker restraining me. The blindfold was another reminder of his hands on me. But Reed's treatment had helped burn away the awful memories of The Mentor's touch upon me. His determination to give me back the lusts that The Mentor had tried to twist had cured me of my fear.

Without Reed's insistence, I wasn't sure if I could have ever allowed a man to touch me after that. I certainly couldn't have allowed a man to restrain me, to encourage me to take back my secret desires to be dominated.

I swallowed and nodded, acquiescing. Reed gave me a gentle smile and slipped the black cloth over my eyes. My panic returned full force when the world winked out of existence, and I pulled against my restraints.

Reed's hand fisted in my hair, stilling my thrashing. "No," he ordered. "Calm down, Katie. You're safe here with me."

I drew in a shaky breath, then another. Slowly, the tension left my muscles as I sank into acceptance.

Reed planted a sweet kiss on my forehead. "That's good. Just be here with me. Relax and feel what I'm doing to you."

I shivered and relaxed further. What he offered was too appealing to fight; to let go, to give everything over to him. And I wanted to give him everything. I wanted him to take everything, to take every part of me, to possess me.

As he had promised, he began his slow exploration of my body, starting at my neck and working downwards. He pressed hot kisses along the upper swell of my breasts, teasing my nipples to aching peaks. I arched my back, silently begging for his attention, but he just laughed.

"Greedy girl," he accused. "I'll torture your nipples when I'm ready."

*Torture?* That wasn't what I-

My thought shattered on a gasp when his tongue traced the lower curve of my breast. Pleasure coiled in my nipples and pulsed in my clit. He repeated the process on the other side, and I writhed against my cuffs, desperate to pull him closer.

"Please, Sir," I begged.

"Since you asked so sweetly." It was my only warning before pain burst across my chest, sending little fissures crackling through my pleasure, splintering it into something more complex.

His teeth sank further into my nipple, and his thumb and forefinger squeezed and tormented the other. Instinctively, I tried to fight him off, but I was securely held by my restraints. He could do whatever he wanted to me, and there was nothing I could do to stop him. The freedom I found in my helplessness was heady, and I moaned my release as I gave in to Reed's will.

His cruel grip eased when he recognized my submission. His growled approval vibrated through my nipples as he eased the pain with his tongue.

He had another reward for me. My vibrator nudged against my opening, and I heaved out a happy sigh as he eased its familiar girth into me. The little rabbit attachment found my clit as he slid it home, and I mewled in pleasure.

His torment of my breasts resumed, alternating between abuse and loving attention. The shots of pleasure and pain heightened my sensitivity at my core, and I came within the space of a minute. The orgasm rocked through me with more force than I was accustomed to with my vibrator, made all the more intense for Reed's ministrations. As I came down, a stinging sensation awoke in my over-sensitized clit.

"Please, no more," I tried to twist away, but the cuffs held me fast, and the vibrator stayed lodged deep within me.

"You're going to come for me again," he informed me, and I could hear the merciless smile in his words. "And again. Until you're quivering and pliant. Then I'll fuck you."

My lustful moan mingled with a sob as his thumb pressed the rabbit down harder against my clit. Despite the discomfort, I came immediately, contracting helplessly around the spinning dildo inside me.

I lost track of the number of times I reached orgasm. Sweat beaded on my skin, and I thrashed and writhed, but Reed's sensual torture continued. Eventually, pain and pleasure blended to one sweet, torturous sensation that ripped ecstasy from my body.

"Please please please," I murmured over and over, and I wasn't sure if I was begging for him to stop or begging for more. After a while, my pleas trailed off to wordless whimpering. My body no longer arched and turned with my orgasms. I could do nothing more than tremble and gasp.

Only then did Reed sweep me up in a fierce kiss. His tongue dominated mine, and in my exhaustion there was no thought of resistance, only sweet compliance. The vibrator left me, and my cry into his mouth was one of loss and relief.

He filled me immediately, driving into my soft, wet heat in one thrust. For the first time, his size wasn't accompanied by momentary discomfort. I was a creature of pure eroticism, and my body was ready to take its master.

I wasn't sure if I came again while he rode me; my mind was so high on bliss that it was no longer able to recognize peaks and troughs. I only knew the deepest sense of satisfaction when he bellowed his pleasure, and his hot seed lashed at me. I drifted off into a sweet delirium, aware of nothing more than his arms around me and the ecstasy of his nearness.

# Chapter 14

The woman who sat before me wasn't the Lydia Chase I had met two months ago. This woman was vibrant, healthy inside and out. Her dark wavy hair was lustrous, and her blue-green eyes shone with a light they had lacked when I first met her. No matter how unconventional their beginnings, her relationship with Smith had obviously been good for her.

"Thank you for coming to talk to me. I know this can't be easy for you."

Her back straightened, her shoulders squaring. "I want to help in any way I can. I'm glad Reed convinced Smith to tell me you wanted to talk to me. I swear, that man would keep me locked up in our apartment if I let him." Her smile was lopsided, as though the idea didn't really bother her all that much. Personally, I found that a bit disturbing, but she seemed happy. I supposed that after what she had been through, a conventional relationship would have been beyond her capabilities.

She seemed to read my discomfiture. "I don't really mean it like that," she clarified. "It's just... Well, you know what our relationship is like," she said it with a little wave of her hand, as though acknowledging her BDSM lifestyle was of no consequence. We had discussed it before when going over her abduction from Dusk, but I hadn't expected her to go back to that life. I guessed I shouldn't have been surprised that the uber-alpha Smith was a Dom.

"And anyway," she continued. "He's just being pushier than usual right now because we're in Chicago and he thinks The Mentor is here. He gets all moody when he thinks I'm in danger." She said it lightly, but I sensed the tension within her. The prospect of one of her tormentors still walking free had to be terrifying. I could hardly believe the woman *didn't* let Smith keep her locked up to keep her safe.

"I'm doing everything I can to catch him. I'm going to find him, Lydia. I promise."

*"Come and find me, pet."* A small shiver raced across my skin.

Lydia's expression turned sympathetic. "I know he's targeting you. Smith told me about the notes. I can ask him to stay here and help you. He knew Martel," her lips twisted with remembered pain. "He'll understand how The Mentor thinks."

"I'm sure he'll want to stay with you in New York. He only brought you to Chicago with him because he wanted to personally speak with Reed, and he wasn't willing to leave you behind. I won't ask him to keep you here while he helps with the investigation. And you know he won't send you back to New York on your own. He's right to worry about you being in Chicago. I have to be honest with you, Lydia; we aren't even remotely close to identifying The Mentor. If he can get to me so easily, he can get to you. You and Smith have to leave as soon as possible."

"Okay, Kate. We'll leave. What did you want to talk to me about? I don't know what more I can tell you, but I want to help, if I can."

"You can call me Katie," I invited. "It's what my friends call me."

She flashed me a brilliant smile. "Katie. What can I do to help?"

My show of good humor was short-lived. How could telling Lydia she could be my friend possibly make up for the horror I was about to make her face? "I have to ask you about The Mentor. I'm sorry."

Her expression became pinched with strain, but her posture remained strong. "I know. And it's okay. I'll do anything I can to bring him down. I won't allow him to hurt any more women."

Her remarkable eyes sparked into mine. "I won't allow him to hurt you, Katie."

"Thank you," my voice was hoarse with emotion. I was deeply touched by her show of strength and compassion, after everything she had been through.

I cleared my throat, forcing myself to focus on the matter at hand. Putting Lydia through this again went against my nature, but I didn't have a choice. "What do you remember about The Mentor?" I began in my best Agent voice. "I know you never saw his face, but can you tell me anything else that might be an identifying marker? Did he have an accent, a particular scent? Anything you remember will help."

Lydia took a deep breath and closed her eyes. Her face went completely blank, detached. When she spoke, it was as though someone else was using her body to say the words. "He spoke like someone who was used to being in a position of authority. He had a broad, Midwestern accent. And he had that sort of scratchiness to his voice men get as they age. Like maybe he was a smoker at one time in his life. He didn't smell like cigarettes, though.

"I definitely got the feeling he was older than Martel. He spoke to Martel like a father figure would. If your father figure was willing to murder you to save his own skin.

"He smelled like expensive cologne, like sandalwood. But underneath that was a rough saltiness, his natural scent.

"He was… Brutal. Cold. It was as though he didn't possess a shred of compassion or any human emotion. He spoke in a bored monotone most of the time, unless he was annoyed with Martel. That was the most emotion I ever heard from him; annoyance.

"Physically, he was fit, muscular. He wasn't saggy or wrinkled, from what I could feel. And he had a big penis. I couldn't say exactly how big. Bigger than Martel."

Nausea gripped me. I couldn't imagine living through that and being able to talk about it. I couldn't imagine being able to go on at all. Much less fall in love.

"Thank you, Lydia. That's a big help."

Her eyes opened, and she blinked, as though she was waking up from a dream. "Is it? I feel like it's not much of anything."

"All the details are helpful. We have an idea of where to look for The Mentor, but we don't have anything to help ID him. Now if we locate a suspect, this will help us know if we're moving in the right direction."

Lydia gave me a weak smile. "I'm glad I talked to you, then. Thanks for letting me help. Smith wants to keep me away from all this, but it's important for me to be involved."

"How do you do it?" I asked in awe. "How are you so strong? How can you-" I stopped abruptly, realizing that I was asking deeply personal questions that had nothing to do with the investigation.

"How can I go on every day after what happened to me?" She finished for me. "Love. Smith showed me that love was still possible for me. I don't think anyone else could have. He has his own unique way of showing affection." Her smile turned wry. "I know you want to ask me about BDSM, Katie. It's okay. Yes, I'm in a D/s relationship with Smith. I was interested in it before I was taken. I think I'm wired for it. It took me a long time to come to terms with that. Then it was turned against me; Martel took me because I could handle pain with sex." Her lips thinned. "But he didn't understand. He took something beautiful and twisted it. Smith smoothed it back out for me. I needed his… *determination*," she half-laughed the word, "to see that what I had always wanted wasn't wrong. Sometimes his support was all that kept me going. He simply wouldn't let me fall. I needed that. I still need it. And not just because of what happened to me."

"D/s is all about trust," I said. "How were you able to ever trust anyone again?"

"Smith didn't really give me an option. It wasn't the healthiest thing for me, from an objective viewpoint, but it was what I needed. He's what I need." Her grin was knowing. "Reed's been talking to you," she surmised. "Good for him. You can trust Reed, Katie."

*D/s is about trust. You can trust Reed.* I connected the dots. My cheeks flamed.

Lydia's hand covered mine. "There's nothing to be ashamed about. Don't waste your time letting embarrassment hold you back. What other people think is right doesn't matter. Only your own happiness matters. Find it how you can."

My phone beeped in the pattern that alerted me to a text message, and I jumped away from Lydia, grateful for the reprieve. Then I checked the text, and I instantly forgot my relief.

*If you keep playing with Carl's toy, I'll have to take her away. You aren't allowed to have toys, pet. You only have me. You belong to me.*

Two seconds of pure terror registered before I responded to the threat. It wasn't just about me this time. I had to protect Lydia. I wasn't going to allow anything else to happen to her.

"Come with me," I kept my voice low and controlled, but she paled.

"What is it?"

"We need to go see Smith and Reed." I didn't want to frighten her, so I kept it to the necessary truth.

Lydia's hands shook as she stood to comply. The men were downstairs in the hotel bar, giving us some privacy but not going too far. They felt too far away now. Even though we were indoors, I felt exposed. Thousands of strangers populated this space. Any one of them could be The Mentor.

As we walked, I positioned my body beside Lydia's in the most protective stance I could manage. I couldn't guard her front and back by myself, but my eyes carefully searched the faces of everyone we passed on our way from the elevator, through the lobby, and to the bar where the men sat.

Reed was instantly on his feet when he took in my expression, and Smith was at Lydia's side in a flash. I quickly showed him the text message.

"Get her out of here," I ordered in a low voice.

"What's going on?" Lydia demanded.

Smith's arm wrapped around her waist, pulling her close to his body. "We're leaving, sweetheart. Now." His expression had turned almost wild. *Moody* didn't even begin to cover Smith James' emotional response when Lydia was in danger. "Call me when you find something," he snapped in Reed's direction. "And keep her safe." He jerked his chin at me and then hustled Lydia out of the hotel.

I glanced at Reed and gestured to my phone. "We need to trace this ASAP." I turned to stride out of the hotel after Smith, but Reed's hand closed around my upper arm, stopping me short.

"Show it to me," he commanded, and I winced. I didn't want Reed to see the text. If he read it, I wouldn't be able to pretend like the only threat was to Lydia. His concern would make it real. I wasn't sure if I could handle it, not after having The Mentor's hands on me.

He had my phone number. It shouldn't surprise me, not after everything else he had done, but it still shook me to my core to have my privacy so flagrantly invaded.

*"I could take you any time I wanted."*

He seemed to know everything about me, and I knew nothing about him.

Reed plucked the phone from my fingers and read the text. As I had feared, his face darkened, and his arm closed around me, just as Smith had done with Lydia. I tried to pull away from him, but he held me firmly.

"We have to go to the field office," I insisted.

"No. We'll get Dex to trace it. You and I are going up to the room and staying there until we know where the text came from." He was already pulling out his own phone to call Dex. I thought about protesting, but I knew he was right. The best thing I could do right now was not engage The Mentor. Staying out of sight was the best course of action.

*I'm willing to allow Reed to keep me locked up to keep me safe.* Ironic, considering I had just been concerned over the fact that Smith did the same thing to Lydia.

But I had seen the dead look in Lydia's eyes just after she was rescued. I had been touched by the same sick bastard who had helped torture her. He wanted to do the same to me.

I didn't at all mind allowing Reed to protect me. All my concerns about losing my strong, independent persona by turning to him for support melted away. They seemed stupid now. Reed had been right. If I kept myself isolated, I was an easy target. Accepting his help – physically and emotionally – only made me stronger.

By the time we were back in the suite and Reed had ended the call to Dex, my lips were tilted in a small smile. His brows drew together in concern when he took in my expression.

"Are you okay?" He asked almost warily, as though he was afraid I was about to lose it.

I wrapped my arms around the back of his neck and answered him with a kiss. He was still for the space of a moment, but then his lips tugged up against mine before his tongue plundered my mouth.

"What was that for?" He asked when I finally pulled back for air.

"Thank you," I said huskily. "For everything you're doing for me. For keeping me safe. For caring. I… I talked to Lydia, and I think I understand things better now. Well, I already understood them, but I'm starting to accept them. Does that make sense?"

Reed grinned. "Not really, but I think I have an idea of what you mean. We're talking about BDSM, right?"

"Yes, but it's more than that. You're helping me to see that it's okay to just be *me*. I don't have to try so hard to be something that's against my nature. I don't want to do this anymore, Reed. I don't want to spend every day looking at pictures of murdered women. I'm sick of the violence and death. All I ever wanted to do was help sick animals, not hunt down sick criminals. And now, thanks to you, I believe Frank never wanted this for me, after all. He wants me to be happy. Lydia told me to find my own happiness." I touched my hand to his cheek. "This is my happiness."

Reed's smile was blinding, and his lips found mine again. When we parted, gasping for breath, he pressed his forehead to mine. Regret filled his dark eyes.

"I wish I could finish this for you. I don't want you anywhere near The Mentor. He wants you to be the one to find him. Maybe if you quit the FBI now, he'll stop targeting you."

I wanted so badly to believe that. "I don't think he will. He seems to actually care about me in some twisted way, and that's not how Lydia described him. I don't know if it's the fact that I'm hunting him that triggered his fascination or if it's something else about me, but this is different. Lydia said he was cold, devoid of emotion. But he told me I make him happy. I don't think he'll stop, Reed. Not until we stop him."

"*We*. I like the sound of that. I'm glad you're not trying to handle this on your own anymore. Thank you for trusting me." His lips brushed my cheek. "We'll catch him, Katie. You'll be safe, and then you can start the life you always wanted."

*What I want is to be with you.* But I was afraid to say what I truly wanted. It was too soon to ask for any sort of commitment. The case would end, and he would be sent back to New York. But if Reed was no longer my partner, then being with him wouldn't be wrong. I could apply to vet school anywhere. I didn't have to stay in Chicago.

*Whoa there, crazy. Just because he likes you and he's sleeping with you doesn't mean he wants anything long-term.* I knew Reed cared about me, but he had probably been with dozens of women. I had only ever dated one other man. I wasn't sure how serious this was for him. It was the most serious relationship of my life.

"What's going on in that busy brain?" He asked.

"I'm just worried..." I chickened out. "I'm worried about The Mentor. We don't know enough about him. How much longer will it be before we take him out?"

*How much longer do I have with you?*

"Don't worry, Katie. I'll keep you safe. We'll catch him soon."

*Soon.* That meant Reed would go back to New York soon. Sadness mingled with relief at the idea of all of this mess being over.

# Chapter 15

"The text came from a burner phone. We can't trace it." Dex's jaw ticked, and he didn't meet my eye. I knew his reluctance to look at me wasn't because of the bad news. He was still angry about what had happened between us in the elevator. When he told me he loved me. When I slapped him.

The sadness that swirled within me didn't match the level of anger I saw surging through every taut line of his body, but it was close. I had gained Reed in my life, but I had lost my best friend. And I wasn't even sure how long I would have Reed. Was it worth losing Dex?

I shook my head wearily. I couldn't change what had happened. I couldn't change what Dex felt for me; what I didn't feel for him.

"Thanks for looking into it, Dex. I appreciate it."

He gave me a stiff nod. The restrained fury in the gesture made my heart twist. Tears stung at the corners of my eyes. I hated what was happening between us.

"I'm sorry I hurt you," I said quietly. I turned to walk away, to escape before I could break down and uselessly beg for his forgiveness.

Iron fingers closed around my wrist, halting my retreat. I turned surprised eyes on him. I hadn't expected violence from him – not against me – but he could easily break my arm if he wanted to. I almost would have welcomed it. At least the physical pain would be some form of penance for the pain I was causing him.

He ground his teeth, saying nothing for a long moment while his pale blue eyes burned into me like the hottest flame.

"I won't let him hurt you, Sparrow," he finally forced the words out through his clenched teeth. "No matter how I feel…. No matter what's happening between-" His fingers tightened around my wrist incrementally. "Nothing else matters but keeping you away from The Mentor. I would never let anything happen to you. You have to know that."

I realized his anger wasn't only directed at me. It was for The Mentor as well. And for himself.

"Thank you," I barely managed to get the words past the lump in my throat. "I appreciate what you're doing for me."

His expression turned impossibly fiercer. "It's not enough. I want you to go to a safe house, but Frank won't agree. He says you're our only chance at catching The Mentor."

My hand found the one that wasn't grasping my wrist, and I squeezed gently. "Frank's right, Dex. I'm his weakness. The more he threatens me, the more he reveals about himself. I'm being careful. I won't go anywhere by myself."

Dex's touch left me instantly, and his face twisted in a mask of pain. "I know you won't," he bit out just before he stalked away.

A fissure crackled across my heart as I watched his stiff retreat. I almost jumped when a strong arm closed around my shoulders in a show of comfort. I breathed in his rich scent, recognizing him instantly.

*Reed.* I turned a small, sad smile on the man who was the source of my joy and Dex's misery.

■ ■ ■ ■ ■ ■ ■ ■ ■ ■ ■ ■ ■ ■ ■ ■ ■ ■ ■ ■ ■ ■ ■ ■ ■ ■ ■ ■ ■ ■ ■ ■ ■ ■ ■ ■ ■ ■ ■ ■ ■ ■ ■ ■ ■ ■ ■ ■ ■ ■ ■ ■ ■ ■

I barely saw Dex over the next week and a half, and a selfish little part of me was glad of that. Facing him was just too painful. The few times we spoke in the office to compare notes, he barely looked me in the eye, and I couldn't seem to quite meet his, either. I found solace in Reed's arms, even as it brought me a trace of guilt.

In that time, our relationship had deepened. That easy companionship I had found with him became the norm. I cherished the hours I spent talking and laughing with him; I felt more free than I had since my father's death. Everything about the new relationship was wonderful. Except carrying out our horrifying task of hunting The Mentor.

I hadn't received any more threats while Reed stayed by my side. We only ever left the hotel to go to the field office. And to get coffee, of course. Reed actually had me drinking the vile stuff. Only, it wasn't so vile, after all. Especially not when it was accompanied by him feeding me bits of pastries to ease the bitter edge of the dark drink. I didn't mind this part at all.

"Open." My lips parted at his dramatically stern order, and he placed the coffee cake on my tongue. His touch lingered on my lips, tracing the line of them before he pulled away. He licked the excess sugar off his fingers with a wicked half-smile. I barely remembered to swallow.

"Now drink." He pressed the warm cup of black coffee into my hands. I tipped it back, and the hot liquid washed over the sweetness on my tongue. It was rich and delicious and dark, just like him.

I gave him a wide grin. "I can really detect the caramel undertones in this blend," I said with an edge of mocking. He took my coffee education so seriously.

He plucked the cup from my hand with an exaggerated frown.

"Hey!" I protested, reaching for it. "I was enjoying that!"

"If you're going to make fun of the process, you don't get your rewards."

"Shhh," I shushed him and blushed bright red. We were alone in the break room, but that didn't mean his voice wouldn't carry out into the office.

He took a step toward me, closing the distance between us so that his body was an inch from mine. He lowered his voice. "Are you sorry?" His eyes sparkled. He was enjoying the edge of danger that accompanied flirting in the middle of the field office.

"Reed!" I hissed, pressing against his chest. "Anyone could walk in here!"

"Are you sorry?" He asked again, holding the coffee cup out of my reach.

"Yes! Yes, I'm sorry." I pushed at him harder. I might as well have been shoving against a rock.

His lips twisted up in a roguish grin. "Try again."

My entire body heated with my embarrassment, but I was getting caught up in the erotic danger of his little game. "I'm sorry, Sir," I whispered.

"Good girl," he murmured against my lips just before stepping away. My chest rose and fell more rapidly than usual, but he appeared nothing more than coolly amused. His grin was still in place when he handed the coffee cup back to me. He picked up the coffee cake.

"Now, let's try that again."

■■■■■■■■■■■■■■■■■■■■■■■■■■■■■■■■■■■■■■■■■■■■■■■■■■■■■

An hour later, my body still burned from our teasing game, and the smirks Reed kept shooting my way let me know he was still thinking of it, too. But as we neared the debriefing room, his usual easy joy deflated. He was practically grim by the time we reached our destination. Just before we entered the room, he schooled his features into a gentle but professional expression. I struggled to match it.

Sitting alone on the couch in the middle of the room, the woman seemed smaller than her five foot five frame should appear. There was a frailty about her that was undeniably haunting. Her auburn hair was streaked with brittle white strands, and there was something… *off* about her deep green eyes. Like an essential piece of her soul had been gouged out.

Kathleen White Parker was still pretty in her own way, but her fine-lined, delicate features only added to her sense of fragility.

She was one of the few women we had identified who had been found alive after her abduction and rape. She had been kidnapped back in 1978, but her case file described being held in horrific circumstances and raped repeatedly by a madman. It was the closest we had come to a lead in weeks.

"Kathleen," I began, using her first name to facilitate familiarity.

"Kathy," she corrected me.

All the blood drained from my face as my eyes roved over her again. Reddish hair; green eyes; pale skin. *Kathy.*

I shared those physical markers. And Katherine and Kathleen could both be shortened to Kathy. Certainty settled in my gut. This was *his* Kathy. This was who he wanted me to be. The one woman who had gotten away from The Mentor.

But I had to be sure.

"Kathy," the name almost stuck in my throat, but I managed to get it out. "I need to ask you some questions about your abduction. I know it was a long time ago, but it will help us with a current case. Would you be willing to talk to us?"

Her eyes flashed with the first true show of emotion I had detected in them. "I…" She hesitated, and for a moment I feared she would refuse. "Yes. I'll talk about it. What do you want to know?"

I hesitated. Truthfully, I didn't want to know. I didn't want to hear the horrors she had been through. Reed covered my silence.

"We've read your file, Kathy," he said smoothly. "But we need to hear some things again. Can you tell me what happened when you were taken? How did he do it?"

"He… I was leaving the library at Notre Dame that night. I never saw him come at me, but he covered my mouth and nose with a rag he had soaked in something. I lost consciousness, and when I woke up, I was There." She said *There* as though it was an official place, an important landmark. I supposed it was one of the most significant places she had ever been in her entire life. Terribly significant.

"Where was 'There'?" Reed asked, picking up on the weight of the word.

She closed her eyes. Unlike Lydia's detached expression when she recalled her abuse, Kathy's was strangely serene. "I think it was a basement. There were no windows, and the only door was up a flight of stairs. The floor and walls were concrete. There was only a bed in the room."

"Were there any other defining characteristics?" Reed pressed. "Anything that might indicate where you were? Do you think you were in the city? Suburbs?"

Her eyes remained closed as she mentally stayed in that place. I wondered at how she could stand thinking about it without any outward sign of distress. Years of therapy must have helped her cope. Our records showed that she was married. Maybe love had healed her just as it had Lydia.

"I'm not sure," she answered. "He told me no one would hear me scream, and no one ever did. He smelled like salt and earth, like maybe He worked outdoors, so I've always guessed it was somewhere rural. That's as far as I've gotten in figuring it out. I never saw anything outside the basement, and even that I didn't see often."

"You didn't see it often? What do you mean?" I asked. I had a feeling I knew exactly what she meant, and it filled me with dread.

"He always kept me blindfolded if He wasn't with me. And He kept me restrained to the bed so I couldn't take it off or even touch anything while He wasn't there. The world didn't exist when He wasn't there." Her voice turned quiet, and I noticed how every time she said *He*, the word was spoken with special significance.

"You didn't know his name," Reed drew the same conclusion I did.

She shook her head. Her eyes remained shuttered. "He made me call Him Master. That's all I ever knew Him as."

The way her face remained so calm disturbed me on the deepest level. There was something inherently wrong with the lack of tension in her body.

*"You'll come to love me,"* The Mentor had told me. Is that what had happened to Kathy? Had he twisted her that thoroughly? *Stockholm Syndrome,* I recognized. That didn't make it any easier to look at her almost beatific expression.

*"This is how I'll keep you. Restrained, blind."* Kathy's description of how The Mentor had kept her blindfolded and tethered to the bed matched how he had held me down when he attacked me in my hotel room.

"Can you describe his demeanor?" I heard myself ask, my voice strangely detached.

"He was harsh, unyielding. Brutal." Kathy maintained her calm. "But He could be tender, too. He would hold me and tell me I was beautiful. He told me I made Him happy."

*"You're very brave. That makes me... happy."* I remembered the surprise and pleasure in the word.

*The Mentor isn't fascinated with me because I'm the one hunting him,* I realized. *He wants me because I remind him of her.*

"How did you get away?" Out of the corner of my eye, I noticed Reed watching me with concern, but I pressed on with my questioning. I had to know more.

The lines around her closed eyes deepened. "He drugged me one day, and then I woke up on my sister's front lawn. I didn't escape; He sent me away."

"Why? Why would he do that?"

"A man came looking for Him, and he found me in the basement. The man tried to rape me, but He saved me. He killed the man. After that, I told Him I loved Him. That's why He let me go," she finished on a whisper. Her eyes snapped open. "I... I've never told anyone that before." She sounded almost surprised.

"We appreciate your honesty," Reed stepped in when I didn't speak. I couldn't have opened my mouth without being sick.

"He's still out there, isn't He?" She asked. "You're trying to find Him." It wasn't a question. She knew.

"Yes," Reed said. "He's still hurting women. One recently escaped, but you're the only other victim we've found alive."

She flinched, and her face fell with grief. "Oh." She seemed at a loss for anything else.

"We have a sketch that was worked up in 1978 based on your description. We'll be able to enhance that for age. This is very helpful, Kathy," Reed encouraged.

"That sketch isn't accurate. I... I couldn't get it to come out right. I never could describe Him properly. After He let me go, my brain started to block it all out. I could just remember a few things; wheat blond hair, amber eyes. He was handsome, I remember that much." She shook her head slightly. "I'm sorry I couldn't do better. I'm sorry other women were hurt." Sadness gave way to determination. "I'll do anything I can to help you find Him."

"Thank you," Reed's voice remained smooth and warm, "This has been very helpful, Kathy."

*Kathy.*

*"I told Him I loved Him."*

The room suddenly seemed far too small. All my focus honed on the woman sitting in front of me.

*Red hair. Green eyes. Pale skin.*

*"You'll come to love me."*

"Katie." Reed's hand found mine, and I jumped at the contact. My eyes snapped to his dark ones, and they pulled me back to him, away from my panic and burgeoning terror. His gaze shifted back to Kathy, but his grip remained firm around my fingers. "Thank you, Kathy. Will you excuse us for a moment?"

"Of course," she eyed me curiously. I knew my professional front was crumbling. I had to get away from her before I fell apart completely. Not only could I not risk distressing her with my own fear, but there was something about her that upset me deeply. Her calm in discussing what she had been through was far more disturbing than Lydia's vacant eyes had been the first time I spoke to her.

I allowed Reed to steer me out into the short, empty hallway. The sunlight that drifted in through the floor-to-ceiling windows helped allay the sensation of being trapped that had assailed me in the small office, but I was still teetering on the edge of panic.

"Reed..." His name was a helpless plea on my lips. His muscles coiled with the effort of stopping himself from pulling me into a tight embrace. We couldn't risk that, not at the field office. But his hands grasped both of mine, his hold tying me to him.

"I know," his voice held its own edge of distress. "She's *his* Kathy. And she looks like you. We both read the case file." His features became pinched. "I know what he did to her. He wants to replace her with you. I can tell you know it, too. You can't be anywhere near this, Katie. It's not worth it."

I swallowed back my nausea. "But he could be doing it to some other woman right now. What about her? What about the other women he's taken? They deserve justice." I tried to find that professionally numb place within me, but I couldn't quite reach it anymore. Reed had helped me let go of that asset, and now I was beginning to regret it. "Keeping me in the open is still our best shot at this. I have to find him. I can't hide forever."

Reed's hands tightened around mine. "You won't have to. We just caught our biggest lead yet. We have Kathy's sketch. We know when and where she was taken. You don't have to be involved anymore. I'll protect you."

A chill clung to my skin. "I can't hide from him. He'll find me anywhere. You know he will."

Reed's jaw firmed. "Not if I find him first."

"You can't-" I was cut off by the trill of my phone. Checking the text provided me with a distraction from the argument. The truth was, Reed was only a few words away from convincing me to go to a safe house. But in my heart, I knew what I was telling him was true; I wouldn't be safe anywhere.

I glanced down at the text.

*I've seen how he touches you. I told you he wasn't allowed to touch you. You belong to me, pet. I'm going to have to punish you now.*

Terror spiked up into my throat, and my eyes snapped to Reed's. A small, unnatural circle of light flashed across the wall behind him. *Rifle scope,* I recognized the reflection immediately. My scream mingled with the sound of glass shattering as I threw my body into his.

# Chapter 16

I lay atop Reed, covering his body with mine. I couldn't bring myself to look at him, to see the damage. If he was hurt...

Strong arms closed around me, and Reed rolled, flipping our positions so that his weight held me down. Relief that he was alive mingled with a new flood of panic. I tried to shove him off, to cover him again. He didn't budge. Instead, he frowned and pinned my arms, ceasing my struggles.

"Get down!" I shrieked. "He won't shoot me!" He had to understand. So long as my body was in front of his, The Mentor wouldn't shoot again. He wouldn't risk killing me. He wanted me too badly.

"Not happening." Reed's hard gaze forbade my resistance. That didn't stop me from trying to fight him.

My eyes honed in on a red line across his jaw. "You're bleeding!" My brain recognized that it was superficial, but that didn't stop the swell of fear.

"It's just a graze, Katie," his voice was low and soothing. "I'm fine."

"What the fuck is going on?" I registered Dex's furious growl over the whistle of the wind blowing through the circular hole in the window.

I twisted my head back to turn terrified eyes on my friend. "Dex! Get out of here!" I let out a small cry when Reed pushed to his feet, pulling me up along with him. I found myself caged in his arms, cradled against his chest. His back was to the window. "Damn it, Reed, stay down! He won't hurt me."

But Reed was already running around the corner, out of view of the shooter. He shoved Dex hard with his shoulder on his way by, driving him out of range with us.

"What the-"

"Sniper," Reed cut Dex off before he could go on a tirade.

My friend was suddenly crowding my body as well, creating a wall of solid muscle around me as we moved deeper into the building. I twisted in Reed's arms, even though it was a useless endeavor.

"You're making it worse! He doesn't want you to touch me. Put me down!" Logically, I knew we were out of view of the window, but I still felt as though his eyes were on me. The Mentor was everywhere, always watching.

Dex shot a glare at me over his shoulder. "Don't you dare put her down, Miller."

Reed's muscles corded around me. "He's not watching now, Katie. And even if he is somehow, I'm not putting you down. Stop fighting me."

"I told you, he won't hurt me," I insisted again, but I went still in his arms. "The text. He wants to kill you, Reed. Not me."

His brows drew together. "What did the text say?"

I bit my lip, not wanting to divulge the contents. They would just send Reed and Dex into even more hyper-protective mode. They would keep themselves exposed to cover me, when I needed to be doing the exact opposite.

"Tell him, Sparrow."

"It was the same thing as before," the words tumbled out in response to Dex's stern order. "He said I belonged to him. And he said he would punish me for letting you touch me, Reed."

Dex's shoulders stiffened, and he didn't look back at us.

I turned imploring eyes on Reed. "He's going to kill you. You have to put me down. Please."

His jaw took on a stubborn set. "In a minute. And only long enough to get you in Kevlar. I'm taking you to a safe house."

I fisted my hand in his shirt. "Then you're coming with me. And you're staying there."

"Katie. If he does want to hurt me, then I'm not staying anywhere near you. Dex can take you-"

"She's right," Dex cut him off. "Both of you need to go. I'll look into the text and the sniper. I have to go get on it right away. We might be able to catch him if we act fast." It seemed to take a great deal of effort for him to turn to face Reed. "You get her to safety." He looked pained saying the words, and I knew he wanted to be the one holding me, protecting me. I broke from his gaze. I was already about to come apart at the seams without guilt and grief over Dex ripping my heart apart.

Reed nodded. "I'll contact you when we get to the safe house."

"Thank you." The words were meant for both men, for Reed's agreement to stay out of harm's way, and for Dex making him see reason. I closed my eyes and tried to find the numb place at my core. It was cruelly elusive. Reed had destroyed that part of me.

■■■■■■■■■■■■■■■■■■■■■■■■■■■■■■■■■■■■■■■■■■■■■■■■■■■■■■■■

The safe house was a ratty little studio apartment that left a lot to be desired, but it was inconspicuous enough. It wasn't nearly enough to make me feel safe from The Mentor. He had shot at Reed in the FBI field office. He could find me here. He could find me anywhere.

*"I could take you any time I wanted."*

I was more certain than ever that The Mentor was in law enforcement. He had the necessary skills, and he knew exactly how to cover his tracks. He knew where Reed would be in the field office. Could it be someone in our own unit? The thought made my stomach turn. It had been easier to think of him as an obscure agent or member of the police force than one of the people I worked with every day.

I looked over at Reed when he locked the door behind us. He hadn't let my body drift far from his, but I had been careful to keep as much space between us as possible.

*I can't let him touch me. He'll die if he touches me again.*

It was all I could think about; that little flash of light, the feeling of my heart hammering in my chest when I tackled him to the ground. My eyes kept finding the angry crimson graze across his jaw.

*My fault.*

He reached for me, and I took a wary step back. Rather than backing off in the wake of my trepidation, his face hardened and he took a prowling step toward me. Before I knew it, my back was against the wall.

"Reed…" I said his name in the low whine of a cornered animal, but he didn't slow his approach.

He reached out and slowly, deliberately, cupped my cheek in his hand. His thumb brushed along my lower lip, touching me with the confidence of a man who knows he has the right.

I turned my face away. "Don't."

He shifted away from me, and for a moment I thought he was going to back off. Then he bent and his arms closed around me. The world tilted, and I found myself staring at the floor. Reed had slung me over his shoulder.

"Put me down!" I tried to kick out at him, but his arm closed around the back of my calves.

"Don't even think about punching me," he warned before I could do just that. I didn't want to truly hurt him, but a punch to the kidney would do less damage than a bullet to the brain.

"I'll do what I have to to keep you safe," I warned.

But before I could fight my way out of his hold, he flipped my body again. When the world settled back into place around me, I found myself draped face-first over his knees where he sat on the edge of the bed. In the next second, he deftly unzipped my slacks and yanked them down to my thighs, taking my underwear down along with them. His other hand caught up my wrists and pinned them at the small of my back.

"What are you doing?" I cried. I jerked and twisted, but there was nothing I could do against him in this position.

His palm swiped over my exposed bottom in a soothing motion. "I know you're scared," he said in a low, even voice, as though he was talking to a spooked horse. "And I know you think you're protecting me by putting distance between us. But I won't allow that."

Pain flared on my right cheek, and I let out a shocked gasp. Reed had never spanked me before. Not like this. There had been playful swats during foreplay, but he hadn't disciplined me.

"Please," I begged. "You have to stop. We can't do this anymore. He'll know-"

The second resounding *crack* of his hand on my ass brought another burst of pain. "I don't care if he knows. I'm not leaving you, Katie. And I'm not going to let you push me away because you're scared." *Crack!* "I'm not going to stop until you accept that." *Crack!* "I won't stop until you accept that I'm going to take care of you."

His tender words contrasted with the sharp pain he gave me. Each hit was hard enough to propel my entire body forward. It made my clit rub against his thigh. Even through my fear and confusion, desire began to pulse within me. My inner walls contracted with every slap, and the heat that arose on my enflamed skin seeped through my flesh and into my core. I knew I should protest. It was so important that I protest. Reed couldn't touch me. He couldn't...

But he was touching me. And he wasn't showing any signs of stopping. His hand came down on me mercilessly, wringing pain and that strange searing pleasure from me. Tears trickled down my face with my frustration and from the harsh sting of his discipline.

Despite my resistance, my will began to bend to his. Even when he was giving me pain, the sensation of Reed's hands upon me was too sweet to give up. He wasn't going to allow my tormentor to tear us apart.

I was ready to accept that. I had to accept it, because Reed had taken the responsibility of choosing out of my hands. Even though my fear for him didn't fully melt, I felt stronger for taking the pain he gave me. I had thought I was protecting him by pushing him away, but we needed to work together to keep each other safe. Divided, we were easy targets. Together, we could watch each other's backs. Reed would stand by me, no matter what.

The tension left my muscles as the fight went out of me. The steady rhythm of Reed's hits stopped instantly. His fingers traced light, swirling patterns over my burning skin. I shuddered as my pleasure spiked at his soothing touch.

"That's good, Katie," he rumbled his approval. His fingers dipped between my thighs and found the wetness there. "Very good." He teased around the edges of my labia, stroking me lightly, but not touching me where I craved it most. He came so close to my clit, but then retreated. I whined out my protest as lust overtook me.

"You want me to touch you, don't you?" He slowly penetrated me up to his first knuckle, but went no further.

"Yes! Please, Sir. I want you to touch me."

He eased in to the second knuckle, and I moaned out my frustration.

"I want you to call me Master."

*"He made me call Him Master. That's all I ever knew Him as."* Kathy's words snaked through my mind with insidious effect. I stiffened in Reed's hold. I wanted to give him what he asked. I wanted to belong to him. But the idea of belonging to anyone when The Mentor wanted to own me made my stomach turn. Reed sensed my discomfiture, and his hand left my sex. His grip closed around my waist, and he turned my body so that I was cradled in his arms rather than being draped across his lap.

"Hey," his gorgeous face was twisted with concern. "What happened? Talk to me."

"I… That's what he made Kathy call him. The Mentor made her call him Master." I shuddered. "I could tell by the way she talked about him that she still thinks of him that way."

Reed's palm touched my cheek, and his thumb hooked below my jaw, holding my face so that I had no choice but to look up at him. His black eyes were intense, filled with a mixture of anger and hunger. "I do want to be your Master, Katie. But I want to be *your* Master. I don't want to make you into something you're not. I want you just like you are. I want to protect you, to take care of you. And yes, I do want you to belong to me. Because I already belong to you."

My breath caught in my throat. "What?" The word escaped me on a tiny puff of air.

One corner of his lips tugged up in a lopsided smile. "I want you to be my submissive, Katie. I want you to be mine."

My head spun. "Your submissive. Is that like… Are you asking me to be your girlfriend?"

His smile turned wicked. "Among other things." His free hand returned to my pussy, playing though the wetness that still lingered there. "Is that something you want?"

Renewed lust shot through my sudden joy. "Yes," I gasped out. "I want that… Master." I added the title with apprehension, as though saying it aloud would call The Mentor's attention to us. He had already proven his jealousy at Reed's hands on me. What would he do to him if he knew about this?

Reed's fingers teased around my clit, calling me back to him with a shot of pleasure. "Say it again," he commanded. "What do you call me when we're together like this?"

"Master." This time, the word didn't waver with fear.

"Good girl." His fingers drove into me in reward. He found my g-spot immediately. "Come for me. Come for your Master." His lips came down on mine, and his thumb rubbed practiced circles over my clit. I cried out my orgasm into his mouth, brought to climax by his heated order and his skillful touch.

Even as I contracted around him, I needed more. As he stroked me through the final aftershocks, I broke from his kiss. "Please fuck me, Master," I whispered against his lips. I rotated my hips, rubbing my sore ass against his hard cock. It jerked, and he groaned.

"Fuck, Katie. I like hearing my name on your lips." He took them again, as though to taste his new title with his tongue.

I gave a small, surprised squeak when he tore his mouth from mine and shifted my body so that I was positioned on my hands and knees on the bed, facing away from him. My pussy pulsed, loving how he so easily manhandled me. After years of training to fight men, it was so sweet to just allow myself to feel carnally vulnerable to a man's strength.

The cool air was electric on my exposed, abused ass. The rest of my body was still fully clothed, only heightening the sensation against my heated skin. Goosebumps pebbled my flesh, even as need caused heat to surge just beneath the surface. My hips rocked back towards him of their own accord, urging him to take me.

His low growl was accompanied by the sound of his belt unbuckling and his zipper being pulled down. It seemed I wasn't the only one who wasn't willing to wait to take the time to get undressed. I shot him a lustful grin over my shoulder, and he returned my smile with a sharp one of his own as he removed his tie. I watched as he tied a knot halfway down its length.

He leaned forward and pressed the silky fabric against my lips, and when they parted, the knot settled firmly between my teeth. I expected him to tie off the makeshift gag, but he kept the ends of the tie loose in his hand. His other arm snaked under my hips and dragged my body back into him. My cry as I was impaled on his cock was smothered by the knot.

His hand came down on my aching ass, and I clenched around him. His soft laugh rippled over me like a palpable thing. His grip on the ends of the tie tightened, pressing the gag back into my mouth until the pressure between my lips forced me to shift my body further back onto his cock. He held me there for a moment, my head pulled up, back arched, trapped against him. He pumped into me once, twice; then held me still again.

"I'm your Master now, Katie. That means I own every part of you," he explained in a low voice. He pulled out and pressed his cock against my asshole. "Every part."

My whimper into the gag was one of fear, but he held me firmly in place with his grip on the tie. He had stretched me there with his fingers while he fucked me, but he had never taken my ass. No one had. I clenched.

He spanked me in reprimand. "You will not keep me out. Relax." His fingers reached around to find my clit. It was still hard with need, and pleasure lanced through me at his touch, despite my fear.

"This will hurt at first, but it can be enjoyable if you accept it. Accept me, Katie." He tweaked my clit, giving me a little shot of pain amidst the pleasure. That unique hit of erotic sensation sent desire crashing through me once again, pushing away my apprehension. My muscles gave slightly, and Reed pressed into me. I hissed at the burning pain as his cock head stretched me, and I tightened again. I tried to squirm away, to escape him, but his hold on the tie was merciless, and his hand cracked across my thigh.

"Relax," he scolded.

His correction did something perverse to my mind and body. Instead of anger or fear, it awoke a wash of lust. He wanted to take my ass, and he would get what he wanted. I had accepted him as my Master, and now he wanted to master every part of my body.

I wanted to give it to him, but it *hurt*.

His hand stroked down my back as he recognized my willingness. "That's it."

I shivered, and he eased in another quarter inch. His fingers found my clit again, eliciting a ping of pleasure from the little bundle of nerves. "The worst is almost over."

He pressed forward ruthlessly, and I cried out as his head passed through my tight ring of muscles with a little popping sensation. He paused there, never stopping his stimulation of my clit.

A string of animalistic whines left me on each shallow breath. The bliss he elicited from my clit danced with the burn in my ass to create something darkly erotic. It was so intense that I wasn't sure I could handle it. But I couldn't have escaped him even if I wanted to. Not only did the tie between my teeth keep me trapped against him, but the nearly overwhelming pleasure/pain he inflicted upon my body immobilized me.

When I acknowledged the fact that I had no desire to escape his sweet torment, the burning turned to something more complex than discomfort. It fed off the pleasure that thrummed from my clit to incite a fire at my core. An orgasm began to build within me, and Reed urged it on, determinedly stroking me toward the precipice.

My scream of pleasure as I came sharpened when he began to slide further into my ass, the way eased by my own wetness on his cock. My head thrashed back and forth, but I couldn't so much as inch away from his steady onslaught while he held me in place with the tie. It was too much. Surely my mind would shatter from the carnal assault on my senses.

My clit was stinging, over-sensitive from my orgasm, but he didn't relent in his stimulation of the little abused bud. He coaxed it back to life, pinching and rubbing until it was hard and needy again. When pure pleasure began to pulse in time with his touch, he rocked his hips back ever so slightly before shifting forward again. The pumping motion awoke a whole new set of nerve endings I had never known existed. I couldn't manage more than a gasp as stars popped behind my eyes. His low chuckle rolled through me, stoking the heat inside.

"I told you you would like it," he said. Although his voice was tight from the effort of holding himself back, it was still saturated with smug satisfaction.

He pumped his hips again and pinched my clit hard at the same time. I screamed out the ecstasy that slammed through me. As I fully relaxed around him, his thrusts increased in speed and intensity, until he was driving in and out of me in earnest. My fingers curled into the sheets beneath me, as though that was the only thing tethering me to the real world.

I could hear him sucking in air in harsh gasps as he altered the way he fucked me. He pulled almost all the way out and stilled. Then he tugged back on the tie, urging me to thrust back towards him. I obeyed, and he let out a satisfied grunt as he began pulling on the tie in a steady rhythm, guiding me to fuck him at the speed he wished.

His complete control over my body, my will, pushed me over the edge again. The release I found in my submission, in his complete domination of my entire being, brought me to bliss. When I began contracting around him, he let out a harsh shout. I felt him pump within me, branding me with his heat. Satisfaction flooded my senses along with my pleasure. We were bound now. I belonged to my Master, and he belonged to me.

# Chapter 17

"How does this work?" I couldn't quite meet Reed's eyes. Instead, I kept my cheek pressed against his bare chest, watching my fingers trail over the contours of his ripped abs. I still wasn't clear on exactly what it meant to be his submissive.

"How does what work?" His voice was a lazy drawl, sated and satisfied. He had fucked me again after we showered together. All I wanted to do was pass out, but I needed to know where I stood with him.

"Us," the little word was tentative. I liked the feel of it on my tongue far more than was healthy. I glanced up at him, hoping my yearning wasn't too pathetically obvious in my eyes. But when I met his, I found a depth of satisfaction there that matched my own. Light danced off them like starlight on a dark pool. I wanted to drown in those warm waters.

"Well, what do you want to do when you quit the FBI? You could move to New York or I could request a transfer to Chicago."

My jaw dropped. "Are you asking me to live with you?" I could hardly believe it. We hadn't known each other very long at all. Even if he was my *Master* – and possibly my boyfriend – living together was a huge step. One that I'd never taken.

He shrugged. "Not if you don't want to. But I'd like to be in the same city. New York is great, but I'm in a position to transfer now since I've been sent here on this case. It would make sense to put in the request sooner rather than later."

"You hardly know me," I marveled. "Why would you do that?"

"Because you're my sub. I want to be close to you. Otherwise, how will I know whether or not you're behaving yourself?" He winked at me, as though this was no big deal.

"Besides, I do know you." His fingers trailed from the hollow at my throat to rest just above my heart. "You're sweet and funny and in need of someone who can help you be your true self. Being submissive doesn't mean you're weak, but your nature has allowed other people to push you down a path you don't want. That doesn't mean they were wrong to do it, just that you put what you thought would make them happy ahead of your own desires. I'll always put you first, Katie. And I'll make sure you put you first."

"But why would you do that for me?" I pressed again, still bewildered.

"Filling that role completes a vital part of me. D/s isn't just about control for me. It's about being needed. After what my father did, after losing my mother… I was alone and angry for a long time. I need to feel that I'm essential to you. Maybe that's selfish, but the truth at the heart of it is that I need you, too."

I touched my fingertips to his cheek, and he leaned in to me. "I do need you, Reed. Despite everything that's happening, when I'm with you, I'm happier than I've been since my father died. I can see a whole new life for myself, and the thought of it doesn't make me sick inside. I want to go to vet school." I took a deep breath and committed. "I'll apply to schools in Chicago and New York. That can make the decision for us."

"Excellent," he grinned, as though the entire situation was settled.

"I still don't really understand what it means to be your sub," I admitted. "You said it's like being your girlfriend?"

"It's better than being my girlfriend, because we get to have wild, kinky sex." He ground his hips up into me, and I felt his cock stiffen.

"So you'll tell me what to do all the time?" I frowned. He was bossy during kinky sex. I wasn't sure I wanted that in my everyday life.

His expression softened. "Of course not. I'll only ever be completely in charge in the bedroom. But I will be firm with you if I think you're doing something that will be harmful to you, physically or emotionally. I'll never force you to do what I think is right in situations like that, but I will be… *persistent.* I want to take care of you, Katie, in more than just a sexual capacity. Is that something you think you could be okay with?"

"Yes, I'm okay with that. It's what I want. You've already done so much for me." I planted a soft kiss of gratitude on his lips.

"Good." His brilliant smile returned. "Now that's settled, we can get back to the fucking part."

My eyes widened. "Again? Don't you need sleep? You were shot today."

"Almost shot," he corrected. He pulled me closer and nipped my lower lip. "And why would I sleep when I have you in my bed?"

A knock rapped against the door, and I jumped away from him.

"Just a-" the latch clicked back, "minute." The last word was a terrified squeak as the door eased open. I jerked the covers all the way up to my chin, as though hiding my body would hide the fact that I was naked in bed with Reed. *Shit shit shit!*

All my frantic embarrassment turned to pure, numbing horror when the intruder was fully revealed.

"Frank," my lips formed his name, but no sound came out. His features twisted to something dark and terrifying, and his eyes were hot enough to consume Reed with fire if he glared for two seconds longer. Usually so implacable, Reed tensed beside me. He knew we were in deep shit.

"Get your hands off her," my father figure's voice was low and controlled, but his hands were clenched to fists at his sides. "You have one minute to get dressed and get out of here, Miller."

"You can't do that!" I cried, even as Reed started grabbing up his clothes. He might be an alpha male, but he wasn't stupid enough to stay naked in bed with a woman while her dad was staring him down. "The Mentor will kill him if he leaves the safe house!"

Frank didn't look at me. "Not if he's in New York. I'm shipping you back to Kennedy tonight, Miller. I'll let him deal with you."

"Frank, wait!" I couldn't allow him to take Reed away from me. "We aren't breaking any rules."

His furious gaze turned squarely on me for the first time. The force of it ripped the air from my chest. "You're breaking *my* rules."

Reed was fully dressed. He was going to leave me. He leaned down and dared to brush a kiss across my lips.

"This doesn't change anything," he told me firmly. "You stay at the safe house. I'll keep working the case remotely." The tension in his face told me it was killing him to leave me alone in Chicago, but he couldn't defy Frank. Not if he wanted to keep his job. And without his job, he wouldn't have access to the information he needed to hunt The Mentor. "Dex will help out here," he assured me.

"Dex will do what I tell him to do," Frank snapped. "I'm not letting either of you near her. You think I don't know what Dex wants from her? I'll work with her personally until this case is over."

Reed squared his shoulders. "Katie is a woman. She can make her own decisions."

"Get out!" It was the first time Frank had raised his voice. He collected himself immediately, but rage still boiled through his words. "If you're not out of Chicago within the hour, you'll find there's not a position waiting for you at the New York field office by the time you get back."

"Frank! Stop it! You're not being fair!" I sounded like an angry teenager who was being told she couldn't go to prom.

His attention returned to me. His eyes were hard, forbidding. The light in them told me he knew what was best for me. "I'm doing this for you, even if you don't see it. You can't have relations with your partner. It clouds your judgment. You could have been shot today trying to protect him. I won't allow that kind of reckless behavior to get you killed."

"But he would have died if I hadn't pushed him out of the way!"

"If he cares about you so much, then he should have died to keep you safe. He's not good enough for you." His glare returned to Reed, who stood stiffly at my side. "Leave. Now."

Reed's eyes were pained when they turned to mine. "I have to go, Katie. But I meant what I said. This doesn't change anything between us." He gave my shoulder a light squeeze. "I'll call you when I get to New York."

With that, he strode away from me. His shoulder brushed Frank's as he stepped past him, not in a show of overt aggression, but he was clearly asserting himself by not skirting around my dad.

When he was gone, Frank turned away from me. "Stay here tonight. I'll come by to pick you up in the morning." He didn't look back at me, but his voice softened. "You'll thank me for this one day. He's not right for you."

*You don't think anyone's right for me.* I kept the petulant words locked behind my lips. I knew if I released them, they would heave out on a sob, and I didn't want to cry in front of Frank. Especially not when I was naked beneath the sheets. Naked and alone. Mortification and grief and anger all swirled within me, a rising tide that came leaking out from the corners of my eyes.

■■■■■■■■■■■■■■■■■■■■■■■■■■■■■■■■■■■■■■■■■■■■■■■■■■■■

The next morning, my eyes were red-rimmed from crying, but Kathy didn't comment on it when I stepped into the interrogation room. I didn't like having her in here, holding her like she was a criminal, but Frank wanted to watch through the one-way mirror. He wanted to see her reactions to the photos I was about to show her.

After Kathy had told us about The Mentor killing a man, Frank had compiled a list of men who had been reported as missing in and around Chicago in 1978. Now he wanted me to see if Kathy could ID any of them as the man who had tried to rape her before The Mentor had murdered him.

I found it sick that she thought of The Mentor as "saving" her from her attacker, when he was the one who raped her repeatedly and broke her mind. But I had to work with what I had, and Kathy was our one solid link to The Mentor.

"Thanks for coming in, Kathy," I said as I settled down across the table from her. "I'd like you to look at a few photographs for me. We're trying to identify the man who assaulted you. The man who your captor killed."

Kathy leaned forward, her eyes sparking with new life as they honed in on the file I placed on the table. Her tongue darted out to wet her lips. It was a nervous gesture, but there was something eager about her posture. "I'll do anything I can to help you find Him."

I suppressed a shudder at the emphasis she placed on *Him*. Even after all these years, she couldn't see him as an ordinary man. He was a twisted, sadistic man, but a man nonetheless. The way she spoke about him made him seem like some kind of god.

I flipped open the file and pushed it toward her. "Are any of these men familiar?" The photographs had that slightly faded look of the era, and some of them were grainy images, cropped and blown up from family photos. Her green eyes skated over the faces, pausing at some to consider more carefully. There weren't many to study. After a minute, she stopped and pointed to the face staring back up at her from the CPD mug shot. The man had been arrested in 1976 for domestic violence.

"Richard Kimbrell," I identified the man. "Does that name sound familiar?"

Kathy shook her head. "I never heard his name. He was only with me for a few minutes when Master came back and pulled him off me." Her eyes glassed over at the memory.

*Master.* This time, I did shudder. The movement brought her out of her reverie, and she blinked. She leaned away from me and crossed her arms over her chest, her stance becoming almost defensive.

"That's the man He killed. That's all I know about him."

*Crap.* I had messed up by letting my own feelings show. Reed had helped me see that I didn't have to live the life of a cold hunter, and now I couldn't keep up the act. My heart ached at his distance. He was back in New York now, and I wasn't sure when I would next feel his embrace.

I forced out what I hoped was a neutral, professional smile. "Thank you, Kathy. This is very helpful."

Her lips pursed, and her only response was a stiff nod. There was nothing more for me to do but walk her out of the building and thank her for her time. IDing Kimbrell was a big win, even if I had messed up by offending Kathy.

Frank was gone by the time we stepped out of interrogation, likely off to do more research on Kimbrell. Or he had left so he wouldn't have to face me. Things had been tense and silent between us all morning, both of us full of righteous anger. Just as thoroughly as I thought he had made the wrong call in sending Reed away, Frank was sure he had done what was best for me. It made it that much harder for me to be angry with him. When all this was over, I was going to have a long talk with Frank about not chasing off every man in my life. Especially not Reed. I wanted him to be *the* man in my life.

Once we got to the elevator, I thanked Kathy again and passed her off to a junior agent to see her safely to her car. She had refused a protective detail, but we would at least watch her every step while she was in our field office. After the shooting the day before, all my illusions that I was safe here had evaporated. I wouldn't feel safe anywhere until The Mentor was behind bars for life.

"Sparrow. I need to talk to you and Frank." Dex's hand closed around my elbow, and he ushered me toward Frank's office before I could come up with an excuse to escape him. With Frank on the warpath against the men in my life, it would have been best to keep Dex at a distance.

"Come in," Frank called when Dex knocked on his door. Wisely, he released his hold on my arm before he opened it. Once I was clear of the threshold, he shut it firmly behind us.

Frank didn't even look at me, and his eyes were less than friendly when they met Dex's. "What is it, Scott?"

"I looked into the text Katie received just before the shooting yesterday," Dex said in a thoroughly professional tone, as though Frank wasn't staring him down. "It came from another burner phone. He knows how to cover his tracks."

My shoulders slumped. "He always knows everything." I hated the thought, but it had to be said. "Do we still think it's one of us?" I asked in a low voice.

Dex's jaw clenched, but he kept his attention on Frank rather than me. "I'm almost positive it is. I went over the transcript of Katie's first conversation with Kathleen Parker. She said The Mentor drugged her and she woke up in his basement. If she was abducted from Notre Dame, that means he can't have taken her far for her to have not woken up along the way."

Frank nodded, following his line of thinking. "Kathy just IDed Richard Kimbrell as the man who was killed by The Mentor. He owned farmland close to the university."

"Well, I went back and looked over Lydia Chase's statement. She also reports waking up in Martel's basement, and not remembering anything between then and when she was abducted. He used Acepromazine Maleate on her rather than something like chloroform that seems to have been used on Kathy, but he still couldn't have given Lydia enough to keep her out for a drive from Chicago to New York. Not without risking killing her."

"But he had the van," I interjected. "We found hair and blood in it."

"I think he used the van to transport his victims from Teterboro Airport. It would only be a half hour drive from there to Martel's house. There's a small airport, DeKalb Taylor Municipal, which is an hour's drive from Dusk. There was a flight from DeKalb Taylor to Teterboro Airport the night Lydia Chase was abducted, in the right timeframe. The aircraft was a private jet. It belongs to Kennedy Carver."

I sucked in a breath. *Reed's boss.* Smith had sworn that Kennedy wasn't capable of being The Mentor, but his name was on the client list at Dusk, and now there was a record of his private jet on a flight path from Chicago to New York on the night Lydia Chase was taken.

It could be coincidence. Maybe he had flown into Chicago to visit Dusk that night. But if that was the case, why wouldn't he have told us he was there when she was kidnapped?

"But Kennedy's in New York," I said. "How could he have sent me the notes? How could he have been the one to attack me? And what about the sniper? He's running the New York unit. There's no way he could leave that many times to come terrorize me in Chicago."

"I thought about that too," Dex said. "If it is Kennedy, he must have an accomplice. The Mentor worked with Martel. He might have another mentee."

I paled. There could be more than one sadistic psycho still out there hurting women. What if it didn't end with The Mentor? How many others had he taught?

"I think it's Parnell," Dex continued. "The shooter left a shell casing in the hotel. It had Parnell's print on it."

"This is good work, Dex," Frank praised. He looked from my former partner to me, his eyes taking in my sickened expression. "I need to talk to Katie for a few minutes."

"Of course. Just tell me what you need me to do next."

"I'm not ready to move on Kennedy just yet. Katie and I are going to discuss our next move, and then I'll let you know the plan." It was a clear dismissal.

I longed to follow Dex out of the office. Things were so tense between Frank and me, and all I wanted to do was escape. But where would I run? Not to Reed. Frank had sent him away. And the further I went from other agents, the closer I got to danger. Frank's office was probably the safest place I could be right now.

"What did you want to tell me?" I asked in as confident a voice as I could muster after the door closed behind Dex.

"I already suspected Kennedy before Dex came forward with this evidence," Frank informed me. "But we can't go after him until we're sure. I've been putting together my own file on him. He used to own a farm not far from Kimbrell's. I'm going to go check it out, and I want you to come with me." His hard face softened in a way it only ever did for me. "I don't trust your safety to anyone else."

My head spun. In the space of a few minutes, we had gone from not having a suspect to compiling strong evidence against the director of the New York unit of the FBI.

"Of course I'll come with you," I heard myself say. I wanted to end this, and if answers could be found at Kennedy Carver's old farm, I would go out there with Frank. Even if I did wish I was going with Reed instead.

*Reed.* He had to know. He wasn't safe in New York.

"I just need the bathroom first," I quickly excused myself. I didn't think Frank would approve of me calling Reed to warn him. But if The Mentor was in New York, then that was the last place I wanted Reed to be.

When I got to the ladies' room, I locked the door behind me and pulled out my phone.

"Hi, gorgeous," Reed sounded tired, but he still had a sweet greeting for me.

"Reed, you need to get out of New York."

"What? Why?"

"I think Kennedy is The Mentor. And he has an accomplice in Chicago. It's Parnell. Dex figured it out, and the evidence is there. You can't be in New York. He still wants to kill you."

"Wait. I don't think it's Kennedy, Katie. Smith's right. He's not capable of doing those things. If you knew him-"

"He owns a private jet. It flew from Chicago to New York on the night Lydia was transported to Martel's house. And he's a patron at Dusk. We know The Mentor is one of us, Reed. Please. You have to get out of New York."

There was a pause. "Okay, Katie, say it is Kennedy. That still leaves Parnell in Chicago to threaten you." He let out a low curse. "I never should have left you there. Kennedy can't leave the New York field office without someone noticing, but Parnell could be anywhere in Chicago. The CPD couldn't get any charges to stick even after he threatened you, and they had to cut him loose."

"Frank and I are going to check out a farm Kennedy used to own. It's near Notre Dame, where Kathy was abducted. I really think he's the one, Reed. Please stay away from him."

"I'll stay away from him, because I'm coming back to get you. Send me the address of the farm. I'm on my way to the airport now."

# Chapter 18

"It looks abandoned," I remarked as we drove down the pitted dirt road. Well, it was a driveway, really. But it was at least a five minute drive from the main road to the farmhouse, and the main road itself was nearly deserted. We really had arrived in the middle of nowhere.

*"He told me no one would hear me scream, and no one ever did."* I could see how Kathy's description of her prison could fit this place.

"No one's lived here since the late seventies," Frank answered, gesturing to the overgrown fields.

"Do you think there will be anything left for us to find? You said Kennedy sold this place. Who are the current owners?"

"An older man who lives in the city. We have his permission to enter the premises."

An odd tension built within me, anticipation mingled with dread. I was afraid of what grisly evidence we might find here, even as the growing sense of finality made me hope for an end to this case. Then I could put all this behind me and start the life I had always wanted.

"Listen, Frank," I began almost timidly. "When we catch The Mentor, I want to leave the FBI. I want to be a vet. I hope you can understand that-"

"We can talk about your future later," he cut me off. "Come on, we're here."

I shut my mouth, nervous and a little hurt that Frank had so casually dismissed my dreams. I got out of the car and picked my way across the sparse gravel toward the farm house. To my surprise, it wasn't dilapidated. The fields had fallen into disuse, but the house itself seemed updated to modern standards. The air even smelled faintly of fresh paint, and I noticed that the siding was bright white, as though it had just been re-done.

"I thought you said the owner lived in the city?"

Frank pulled a key out of his pocket and motioned for me to join him on the porch. "He does, but he's planning on moving back out here."

When he opened the door, it swung inward to reveal a thoroughly modern home. There was a brand new plasma TV on the wall and half a dozen laptops set up on the desk in the corner. It was so at odds with the desolate landscape outside the house. I stepped across the threshold.

"Welcome home, Kathy." The voice was deep, with a broad accent. My heart jumped up in my throat, and I whirled. Frank stood there, grinning. I heaved in a deep breath and then let it out in an angry huff.

"That's not funny, Frank!"

He closed the door, his lips still split in a wide smile. It struck me that I had never seen Frank smile quite like that.

"Have you ever known me to make a joke?" Somehow, that stranger's voice came from his lips.

I took a wary step back. "Now is a pretty awful time to start. Stop talking like that."

"This is my voice, Kathy. My real voice. You've heard it before."

"Stop calling me that!" My voice was high with anxiety. Why was Frank acting this way? Why did he sound like... That accent.

*"He had a broad, Midwestern accent,"* Kathy had described The Mentor.

I took another step back, my head shaking wildly from side to side. "I don't know why you're doing this, but I want you to stop. Maybe you're not used to making jokes, but this isn't funny."

"I think it is. This is the most fun I've had in years." His eyes glittered as he reached into his pocket. My stomach dropped when he pulled out a syringe. "I could have taken you at any time, but this is so much better. I wanted you to find me. My clever little pet."

My body acted before my mind could process what was happening. I fell into a defensive stance, and his grin widened.

"And so brave, too. I knew you were perfect for me, Kathy."

"Stop it!" I shrieked. "Stop calling me that!"

He laughed. It was much richer, more genuine, than any laugh I had ever heard from him. "I'll call my property whatever I choose."

I took in a long breath and tried my best for a steady voice. "I'm going to leave now, Frank. Just let me leave, and we'll forget about this."

He shook his head at me, as though I was a child who couldn't quite understand an adult concept. "You're not going anywhere ever again. You belong to me."

His body shifted, ready to lunge. Frank had taught me to recognize the signs of an attack. I twisted out of the way of the jabbing needle and came up under his outstretched arm to catch him in the stomach. He turned his body so that the blow glanced off him, and his free hand made a grab for my shoulder. I dodged away, putting several feet of space between us. His indulgent smile let me know he had allowed it.

I recalled the years of training with him, the hits I had taken from him. He had said they would make me stronger.

His eyes gleamed. "Come on, fight me. Show me what you've learned."

Tears gathered at the corners of my eyes as the last nine years of my life twisted in my mind, becoming something sick and sinister.

"Don't do this, Frank. Just stop it." It was a child's plea.

"No," he reprimanded. "Not Frank. You'll call me Master from now on, pet."

He came at me again, and this time the needle grazed a thin red line across my neck when I jerked away sloppily.

"Come on, now, Kathy. I taught you better than that."

I came at him with a scream of rage. He smiled even as my fist made contact with his jaw. He moved with the punch, minimizing the damage. He would probably barely have a bruise. And I had gotten too close. His arm closed around my upper back, pulling me against him. The needle plunged into my upper arm.

My muscles weakened almost instantly, and I jerked against his hold. He cupped my cheek in his big hand, cradling my face so I was forced to look up at him.

"I've been waiting to see the look on your face when you realize who I really am." Red gleamed through the amber of his eyes. How had I never seen it before? "And there it is. So beautiful."

The visceral horror wasn't enough to keep the darkness at bay.

■■■■■■■■■■■■■■■■■ ■■■■■■■■■■■■■■■■■■■■■■■■■■■■■■■■■

"Wake up, pet. I'm getting tired of waiting." A light slap across my cheek made my brain rattle against my skull. My head throbbed, and my entire body felt too heavy. A sense of dread stirred in my gut, but my mind couldn't quite put together why. I opened my eyes to take stock of my situation.

My vision was black; my lids were securely shuttered by something tightly pressed against them. Panic surged, doubling the pounding in my head but clearing the cobwebs from my thoughts. I tried to rip the blindfold off, but my arms barely moved. I recognized the feel of soft cuffs ensnaring my wrists.

Rough fingertips brushed my cheekbone. "There she is."

That voice was so familiar and yet so *wrong.*

"Frank," his name stuck on my too-thick tongue. I swallowed and tried again. "Please. Why are you doing this?"

"It's *Master*, not Frank." He clucked his tongue at me. "I haven't even explained the rules yet. I'll answer all your questions honestly. But for each one, there's a price. You get to choose how much you give up to me. You just lost your shirt." He chuckled at his sick joke.

Cold steel edged beneath the lower hem of my blouse. "Don't!" I twisted away, and sharp pain flared as the knife nicked my belly. My body went rigid, my muscles not even daring to quiver with my fear. All I was conscious of was the point of the blade against my all-too-delicate flesh. I didn't even breathe as it scratched up my stomach, not quite breaking the skin. When it reached the first button on my shirt, the fabric tugged once before the button popped away. A high, animal whimper escaped me then.

His hand skimmed up my stomach in the wake of the blade, parting the fabric as he cut it open. "I've waited so long for this," he practically cooed. I couldn't see the expression of sick delight on his face. I was almost glad of that. At least this way, the knowledge that the man assaulting me was my father figure was an abstract thing. The Mentor couldn't be Frank if he didn't look like Frank. He sounded different enough that I could almost convince myself.

But then there was the way he smelled; expensive sandalwood cologne, playing over his natural salty scent. My brain remembered Frank holding me while I cried, even as I mentally revolted against the idea that the man violating me was the one I had loved like a dad.

My anguish left me on a piercing scream when the last button gave way. Frank laughed, that rich, genuine laugh I had never heard before today. How had I never realized how cold and stilted his other laugh was?

The blade sheered through my long sleeves, and cool air brushed across my exposed torso. I was still wearing my bra, but I had never felt so naked.

The cold weight of the knife settled between my breasts as he set it down on my sternum. I breathed again, but only out of necessity. Oxygen came in tiny inhales for fear that the steel would shift on a gasp and slice me open.

"You asked why I'm doing this, and I promised an honest answer," his voice oozed over my bare skin. "I'm doing this because you're perfect. I made sure of it. I always knew you were a clever girl, and you had the capacity for bravery. It just took a guiding hand to show you that. The first time you threw yourself into my arms and cried against me, I felt… I *felt*. I hadn't felt anything since I lost Kathy. The other women were just toys. Toys to play with and break and replace. None of them satisfied me. None of them made me *feel*."

His fingers stroked through my hair. I turned my head away in revulsion, but his hand fisted in my curls, pulling me back where he wanted me.

"You'll fight me. You'll try to outsmart me. And if you're very good at the game – which I know you will be – you'll actually manage to surprise me. I know you'll be good at it because I've trained you for this for nine years."

I had no words. I couldn't even formulate thoughts. All that filled my mind was a despairing wail. After a while, I realized it filled my ears as well. I was making the agonized sound.

I forced myself to go quiet. *Think, think.*

But he wanted me to try to outthink him. My stubborn streak told me to defy him, but how could I do that when what he wanted was for me to try to escape him?

*Reed knows where I am. He'll come for me.* I clung to that knowledge, but I wasn't willing to just lie there and wait for rescue. I had to keep him talking. So long as he was talking, he wasn't… *raping me.* I stumbled over the thought.

"They'll find you," I told him with a surety I didn't feel. "Parnell won't keep your secret. He'll give you up to save himself."

There was a long silence. For a few seconds, I thought I had spooked him. Then I detected the disappointment in his little sigh. The truth clicked into place.

"You framed Parnell. Just like you framed Kennedy."

"Very good, pet. They'll never look at me because they'll be too busy trying to unravel the puzzle I left for them."

I pursed my lips. I couldn't ask him how he had done it. A question meant surrendering more clothes.

"Parnell wasn't the shooter," I said carefully. "You were."

His finger tapped the center of my forehead. "So clever. But you don't get something for nothing. I'll tell you how I did it. All you have to do is ask."

I hesitated. I couldn't bare any more of my body to him. It was too sick.

But who knew what he might decide to take if I didn't play his little game? If I made my move, I could at least guess his countermove.

"How did you do it?" The question was so shaky that it was barely coherent.

He plucked the blade from between my breasts, and I heaved in my first proper breath in what felt like hours. But my reprieve was short-lived; the knife's edge eased under the top of my slacks.

"I've been dying to get a proper look at you," his voice was husky, lustful, as he cut my pants away. "Those cameras in your apartment didn't do you justice."

Bile rose in the back of my throat. How long had he been watching me?

But I had already asked my question, and I was paying dearly for it. I cried silently while he stripped me down to my underwear, not daring to make a sound lest I miss one word of his response.

"Kennedy was already conveniently on the list of patrons at Dusk," he began. "It was a simple matter of hacking into DeKalb Taylor's and Teterboro's flight records and swapping my jet for his on the flight that took Lydia Chase from Chicago to New York."

"Your background in ASE&T," I remembered his history in the beginnings of the Applied Science, Engineering, and Technology branch of the FBI before he applied to become a field agent. He would have been trained in forensics, electronic surveillance, and biometrics. If he kept up with advances in those technologies, he would be just as highly trained as current ASE&T Professionals. "You manipulated the cameras when you when you attacked me at the hotel. And when you tried to shoot Reed."

"And I left the casing behind with Parnell's print. Which isn't actually his print, by the way. The bullet was from another case. I switched the print records in the database so it would read as his. By the time the cops figure that out, they'll have another rabbit hole to go down."

My head spun. A background in tech, a high level of weapons training, foresight that made him seem practically omniscient; as the director of the New York unit, Kennedy Carver was the perfect scapegoat.

"This farm," I grasped at straws, trying to find flaws in Frank's plan. "Kennedy used to own it. They'll come to check it out and find me here."

"No. I lied. It never belonged to Kennedy. It's always been mine."

"Dex knows you brought me here. He'll come looking for me."

"I made him leave my office before I told you about the farm, remember? Dex doesn't know where we are. And I've already redirected the GPS signal on your phone to make it look like you're back at the safe house. They'll think you were abducted from there."

"Reed knows," I flung at him. "He's on his way here now. If you let me go, you might have time to outrun him."

"I thought you might tell Miller." The pleasure in his voice made my stomach tighten. "Now I'll finally get to kill him for touching what belongs to me." He stroked my hair again. "Watching you take pain from him when you should have been taking it from me made me… angry." He seemed to savor the word, as though each drop of emotion I wrought from him was precious. "But it just proved to me how perfect you are. I won't even have to train you to find pleasure in pain. It's already ingrained in you."

"No." He was twisting everything Reed and I shared and making it something sick and wrong. Reed had worked so hard to help me get past my fear of wanting pain with sex. He had helped me to see that it was natural, even beautiful. Now Frank made it something loathsome.

"Yes." He traced the upper swell of my breasts, and I gagged from the intensity of my revulsion. "You're my perfect pet. I'll never need another toy. I'm keeping you forever. I'm going to retire once I've tied off all the loose ends. I'll be here with you, always."

There was true tenderness in his voice. Like his laugh, this was a genuine side of him I had never seen before. This was the real Franklin Dawes, a man who was so emotionally isolated that he would commit the most heinous crimes just to feel anything at all. And now he found those emotions through terrorizing me.

*Reed will come for me, Reed will come.* But the hope I found in that certainty was tainted by fear. Frank might kill Reed if he came here. I had to get out of this before he arrived. I couldn't ask another question. Another question would leave me fully naked. I didn't want to contemplate what came after that.

*Think, think.*

*"I told Him I loved Him."* Kathy's words came back to me. Frank had let her go because she admitted her love for him.

"I loved you, Frank." The words weren't hard to say; they were true. What was more difficult was putting them in present tense and purging them of the bitterness of betrayal. "I love you."

The blindfold was ripped from my eyes, and light flooded my vision. I blinked hard, and the world coalesced around me. As I had dreaded, I was restrained to a bed in what appeared to be a basement. There were various apparatuses for bondage scattered throughout the room, a cage in the corner, and chains hanging from the ceiling. My body went into flight mode as fear overtook all my senses, but my arms jerked uselessly at the cuffs.

"Shhh." Strong hands cupped my cheeks, steadying me. The comfort I found in them was horribly familiar. Frank's face appeared above mine, proving that this was all real and not some elaborate trick The Mentor was playing on me.

Frank was The Mentor. Oh, god, Frank was The Mentor.

"Shhh," he soothed me again, brushing the tears from my cheeks with his thumbs. "Don't cry. Tell me again. Look me in the eye and tell me you love me."

"I…" The words stuck in my throat. *If I tell him I love him, he'll let me go.* "I love you," the lie came out through chattering teeth.

His face split into a wide grin. "So clever, my little pet. That was a very good try. But I'm not letting you go this time, Kathy."

"I'm right here, Master." The tremulous voice floated down from above. Kathy – the real Kathy – stood at the top of the staircase that led down into the basement. "You could have had me forever, you know. You didn't have to hurt those other women. You don't have to hurt her."

"Pet," Frank said the endearment with shocked reverence. His expression was tight with yearning as he watched her begin to descend the stairs. "The others never gave me what you did. They screamed, but it wasn't the same."

Kathy reached the bottom of the stairs, and she paused, watching us warily. "Then why do you need her?" She gestured toward me. I was shocked to realize her voice was touched with jealousy.

"I was... empty. Lonely." That was one emotion he didn't seem to relish. "I was only ever my true self when I was with you." His fist tightened in my hair possessively. "I want that again. She can give it to me. I've made her just for that purpose."

Kathy took a tentative step toward him, her eyes flicking to the knife in his hand before lifting back to his face.

"But why hurt her when you could have me?" The question was colored with longing.

Frank's expression shifted to a hard mask. "You were useless to me once you told me you loved me." I recognized his false, cold voice that he had always used with me. "Our games would be meaningless. You would do anything I asked of you because you wanted to make me happy."

Kathy closed the last of the distance between them. He stiffened, but she boldly touched her fingers to his cheek. Her show of tenderness to the monster who hovered above me was both horrific and fascinating.

"You're lying," she said quietly. "You sent me away because you loved me, too. And you couldn't handle feeling that much. I know you, Master. I know your soul. All you want is to not be alone, but you don't understand how to achieve intimacy without inflicting your own pain on someone else. When you took me, you didn't know how to feel anything at all. Your love for me scared you."

He grabbed her wrist in a white-knuckled grip, but he didn't pull her hand away from his face. His features twisted in furious anguish, but Kathy didn't flinch away. She stared up at him with open devotion.

"I've been looking for you for thirty-five years," she whispered. "But you hid from me. You didn't want to love me. When Katie identified the man you killed as Richard Kimbrell, I tracked down where he used to live. I knew it couldn't have been far from you. I found this farm. I finally found you." She pointed toward me, but she didn't take her eyes from his. "Let her go. You don't need her. Take me back, Master. Please. I still love you. I will always love you."

"Stop, Kathy!" I finally broke my disturbed silence. "You can't trade yourself for me. Everything's going to be okay. You don't have to stay here with him. You don't have to suffer any more."

She turned a small, sad smile on me. "I know I don't have to stay. I want to. Master ruined me for anyone else. I have suffered every day since He sent me away. I've lived a half-life without Him." She looked back to Frank, her eyes shining. "You sent me away, but I've never let you go."

His growl was one of hunger and desperation, and his hand left my hair to fist in hers. He pulled her in for a vicious kiss, taking her mouth with such ferocity that her back arched and her head dropped back. They might have seemed romantic in their fiery passion if it weren't for the sick nature of their relationship.

He pulled back from her and snarled against her lips. "Mine. My pet."

Her arms twined around the back of his neck, pulling him closer. "Yes, Master. Yours."

"Katie!" Reed's voice broke the intense moment. His footsteps creaked above the basement. "Katie, are you here?" The question didn't hold the panic it should. He had no idea what was happening in the basement. If he came down here unaware, Frank would kill him. But I couldn't let him leave me here. If Frank had already manipulated the GPS signal on my phone, there would be no record that I had ever been here when Reed went to check it.

"Reed!" I screamed his name. "It's Frank! He's-"

Frank moved faster than I could process. His hand cracked across my cheek, the shock of the blow silencing me. Through watering eyes, I saw him grab Kathy so that her back was pinned to his front. He pressed the length of the knife against her throat.

"Come in slowly and put your gun where I can see it, or she dies," he called out.

Reed's running footsteps slowed. When he stepped through the door at the top of the stairs, his brows were drawn with worry and confusion. Then his gaze fell on me where I was restrained to the bed, nearly naked. I had never seen his eyes go so dark. His gun lifted.

"Ah-ah," Frank chided, and Kathy sucked in a breath when a drop of blood bloomed against the point of the knife. Despite her situation, I was shocked to find that her eyes were devoid of fear; they held nothing but sadness.

"Put your gun down on the ground," Frank ordered.

Reed's entire body tensed, and his nostrils flared with his frustration and fury, but he complied.

"You touched what was mine. You hurt what was mine to hurt." Frank's eyes were fevered with his own anger. "Now come down here so I can kill you with my bare hands." Reed hesitated, his hand twitching back toward where his gun lay at his feet. "If you don't want to watch Kathy die, your only other option is to run. You can run and leave her here with me." He nodded at me and flashed a cruel grin. "But we both know you won't do that. Leave the gun and come down here."

Reed's eyes found mine again, and his resolve hardened. He knew he didn't have any other options.

"I'm sorry," the apology hitched in my throat.

"It's okay," he assured me, his voice carefully controlled. "I'm going to get you out of this, Katie."

Frank laughed. "I might be older than you, but that means I have thirty years of experience on you. And you won't be the first man I've beaten to death." His grin was sharp. "It's my favorite way to kill. I'm very good at it."

My heart pounded against my ribcage, and for a moment, I considered screaming at Reed to run. But if he chose to leave, I would be left alone with Frank. He would take me somewhere else. I knew how good he was at hiding. Reed would never find me again.

He descended the stairs slowly, watching Frank, calculating his next move. As soon as he reached the bottom, Frank flung Kathy away from him and dropped the knife.

"I don't need a weapon to kill you, boy," he sneered.

With that as his only warning, Frank launched himself at Reed. Reed barely moved in time to ensure that the first blow glanced off his jaw. Frank was as fast and experienced as he had claimed, and he fought with murderous intent. As Reed dodged away, I saw something shift in his eyes, wariness morphing to resigned determination. I knew Frank wasn't the only one who planned to kill.

Reed went on the offensive, catching Frank solidly in the gut. He doubled up, and Reed brought his knee up under his chin. Frank dropped and rolled away, narrowly avoiding Reed's kick at his ribs. He swept Reed's legs out from under him, and then the two men were grappling on the ground, each fighting for dominance.

Reed broke away and managed to get to his feet. Before he could kick Frank while he was down, Frank was upright as well. But he didn't have time to deflect Reed's vicious blow, and the sickening crunch of Frank's nose breaking made me shudder. Even after all he had done to me, it pained me to see my father figure being hurt. It was fucked up, but part of me couldn't stop thinking of him as my dad.

Reed spun him around, and his hands braced on either side of Frank's head. He was half a second away from snapping his neck.

"Stop!" I shrieked. "Reed, don't!" I couldn't bear to watch the man I loved kill my father. The dark flames of Reed's eyes found mine. He was high on adrenaline and bloodlust, but he paused. "If you love me, don't kill him."

His hatred melted to something so fervent it made my heart skip a beat. His grip on Frank eased.

There was a scream beside me, and suddenly Kathy blurred past me. Something silver arced through the air, and Frank grunted when she came to a stop before him.

The handle of the knife stuck out from his chest, Kathy's hand wrapped around it.

Reed backed away in surprise, and Kathy caught Frank's falling body. She slowly lowered him to the ground, cradling him to her chest.

"I'm sorry, Master. I'm so sorry." Tears streamed down her face to splash on his. "I couldn't let you hurt anyone else. You should have hurt me. You shouldn't have sent me away."

Frank wheezed in a breath, his eyes wide with surprise and a hint of wonder. He lifted a shaking hand to her face. "My brave little pet. I…" He coughed, and blood painted his lips red. "I love you."

"I love you too," she forced out through her heaving sobs. "But I have to let you go. Goodbye, Master."

"Kathy…" Her name rattled from his chest, and his hand dropped. The reddish light seeped from his eyes, leaving them a dull amber.

She screamed out her agony and pulled him closer, rocking his lifeless body in her arms.

# Chapter 19

"I know you've been through a lot, but I need you to explain what happened from your point of view, Kathy," Dex spoke gently.

"Kathleen," she corrected. Her eyes were red-rimmed, but there was a new confidence in the set of her shoulders, as though a great weight had been lifted from her. "I was Kathleen before he took me." *He* was no longer spoken with reverence, only sadness.

"Okay, Kathleen. Can you tell me what happened?"

I watched through the one-way mirror as Kathy – no, Kathleen – went through the details of how she had located Frank's farm and the terrible events that unfolded in the basement the day before. Reed stood at my side, his arm tightening around my waist as he listened.

"You don't have to be here, Katie," he told me. "Let me take you home."

*And where is home? My tainted apartment? Your hotel room?*

"No. I need to hear this. Look at her, Reed. How is she okay? How is she *better*? I have to know." *I have to know how she's sitting there and talking as though her entire world isn't crumbling down around her. Then maybe I can imitate it.*

"What can we do for you now, Kathleen?" Dex asked kindly when she had finished. "We have a therapist you can talk to."

"I'd like that. Maybe I'll actually try to let them help me this time. I held on to him for so long," her lips twisted with grief. "But I have a family now. A husband and two sons. They've never really had all of me. I never lived the life I wanted, because Master – because Franklin took it from me." Her back straightened. "I think I'll go back to school and get the final credits I need to start a career in marketing. That's what I wanted, before. It's time for me to move on and finally live my life."

Dex smiled at her. "That's very brave of you, Kathleen."

She flinched at the compliment *brave*, but her expression quickly cleared. "Thank you, Agent Scott."

With that, Dex ushered her out of the debriefing room. As she passed me in the hall, her deep green eyes locked on me. They were soft, sympathetic, but she didn't offer any words of comfort. She knew from experience that they would be useless. I had to figure out my own way to piece myself back together, just as she had.

"I have some new intel, if you're ready to hear it," Dex told me gently.

I lifted my chin, struggling to find my cold professional façade. I ignored Reed's frown. "Yes, I want to hear it."

"Just like Frank told you, the fingerprint on the shell casing wasn't actually Parnell's. It belonged to a gang-related case. Colton found the evidence against Parnell that had been lost. It looks like Frank hacked the CPD's database and messed with the records so it seemed to be missing. He wanted Parnell to serve as a distraction. Now we'll be able to put him behind bars, so that's a win."

"That's a win," I repeated in a hollow voice.

Dex eyed me carefully, but he continued. "We ran Frank's DNA. It didn't match what he had on file with the Bureau. He seems to have changed that in the database as well. We don't know whose he used, but when we ran his, there was a hit in the system. Frank was Carl Martel's biological father. I didn't say anything to Kathleen, but we checked it against her DNA, and it looks like she's the mother."

"She abandoned Martel as a baby," I concluded.

"Can you blame her?" Dex asked quietly.

"No, I guess not. Are you going to tell her?"

"I didn't think she had to know. She's been through so much. She doesn't need Martel's crimes on her conscience as well." He shook off the darkness that had entered his eyes. "We aren't sure when or how Martel found Frank, but it seems that Frank worked with him because he was his son by Kathleen. It matches up with the reports from Lydia Chase about how The Mentor spoke to Martel."

"Frank, not 'The Mentor,'" I said dully. "Frank was The Mentor."

Dex reached for me, but his eyes fell to Reed's hand where it was curled around my hip. His hand curled to a fist, and he withdrew it slowly. The flash of anger in his clenched jaw quickly faded to resignation. The sight of it made my heart hurt.

His pale blue eyes met Reed's dark ones. "Get her home. She doesn't need to be here." Reed nodded his agreement and started to turn to leave. "And Miller," Dex added. "You take care of her." The depth of emotion in his voice let me know that he was talking about more than just looking after me because of what had happened with Frank. Dex was letting me go and giving Reed his approval.

"Thanks, Dex," I whispered, peeking up at him cautiously.

His eyes blazed and his fingers furled and unfurled, but he gave me a single, sharp nod. Then he turned and walked away from me. I sensed that he wasn't walking away forever, though. We could heal the rift between us; Dex had proved that much through his approval of Reed. He just needed time. The knowledge filled me with relief that briefly flooded the gaping chasm in my chest.

Reed gave me a gentle squeeze. "Come on. Let's go home."

The black hole where my heart had been yawned open once again. "And where is that?"

"With me," he said firmly. "We'll find a place to live, but I'm your home. And you're mine, Katie."

As much as I wanted to believe that, I couldn't trust it.

"I used to think Frank was my home," I choked out. Tears threatened, and I scrambled for my professional front. I didn't want to fall apart. I didn't want to face the hurt.

Reed pulled me into the debriefing room and lowered the blinds for privacy. As soon as he switched off the microphone, he wrapped his arms around me.

"You don't have to hold it in. It's okay. Cry, Katie." It was an order.

I couldn't resist him. The floodgates opened. "He was my father," I gasped out when the first tears fell. "How could he… do that… to me?" I forced out the words between sobs.

"The man you knew wasn't the real Franklin Dawes. He manipulated everyone around him, you most of all, because he actually cared about you."

"He didn't care about *me*. He made me what he wanted me to be." Anger bubbled up, and I swiped at the wetness on my cheeks. "And I let him. I did everything he wanted me to do because I'm *submissive.* He made me everything I am."

Reed's hands closed around my shoulders, and he held me away from him so he could capture my eyes with his.

"Don't do that, Katie," he commanded. "Don't let him win. Yes, he manipulated you. He took advantage of your good heart. But that doesn't mean there's anything wrong with you. The person you tried to be to make him proud wasn't really you. You constantly struggled to deal with the terrible things you've had to face in your job. Don't let him take your greatest assets from you and make them his. You are smart and brave, Katie. That's in your nature. He didn't make you that way. But it's also in your nature to help, not to hunt. You've been successful at a job you hate because of your dedication to helping the victims, not because you get any satisfaction out of taking down criminals."

I longed for what he was saying to be true, but there was still an uglier truth about my nature that Reed hadn't dared to address. "I would have let him hurt me," the words were barely audible, but they left my lips nonetheless. "And I would have liked it. He told me I was perfect for him, and he was right."

"You *are* perfect, Katie. You're perfect for *me*. I love you for who you are, not who you tried to be to make him happy. And don't you dare say you would have liked it when he hurt you. We discussed this when we first met. There's a difference between abuse and BDSM. You enjoy the pain I give you because you trust me. It allows you release. What he wanted to do to you..." His features drew taut with a flash of fury, but he quickly smoothed it away. "You would never want that. Not of your own free will."

I was beginning to believe his fierce declaration, but my mind caught on one thing in particular. "You love me?"

His brows rose, as though he was surprised at my wonder. "Of course I do. Have I not said that yet?"

Despite everything, a shaky laugh popped out of me. "No, you haven't. I love you too, by the way."

"I know you do."

I rolled my eyes at him, my anguish melting away in the wake of his easy humor. "This is very romantic," I managed a hint of sarcasm.

"Would you prefer if I got down on one knee?"

My breath caught. "Wait. What? This isn't a proposal, Reed. Is it?" I added, a touch hopeful.

He laughed, that rich sound I loved so much. "Do you want it to be? I don't have a ring or anything yet."

"Yet?" Incredulity didn't fully douse my giddiness. "Isn't this all a bit soon? We haven't known each other very long."

He shrugged. "I'll wait and do it properly, then. I might not have known you long, but I know *you*. You're everything I want, Katie. It doesn't matter to me if we get a ring today or five years from now. I've known I wanted you to be with me forever since the day I asked you to be my sub. I wouldn't have asked otherwise. Did you not realize that?"

I threw up my hands in happy exasperation. "How would I know that's what you meant? I thought it barely meant I was your girlfriend."

He shook his head at me, chuckling. "Didn't those BDSM romance novels teach you anything? You called me Master. That means you're mine. I'll get you a collar and a ring if that makes things clearer for you."

I tried my best not to flinch at the title *Master,* but Reed read my sudden discomfiture. His fingers traced my jawline, coming to rest beneath my chin so that I had no choice but to look up at him.

"I understand that everything you went through is still fresh for you, but I *am* your Master, and you'll address me properly when it's appropriate. You remember how I told you I might be firm with you outside the bedroom? This is one of those times. I know this is what you want, and I won't allow what happened to scare you off."

My heart twisted. I wasn't sure if I could ever hear the word Master again without shuddering, much less let it leave my own lips.

"I don't know if I can, Reed."

His lips thinned, and he spoke to me sternly. "You can and you will. But I'll give you time."

"Thank you," I said, even as I doubted him. But there was one thing I had absolutely zero doubts about. "I love you, Reed. And I think I would like that ring. And the collar," the last was a shy admission.

He grinned. "Then it's a good thing I've already picked out both of them."

"You didn't," I said in disbelief.

"I did. I'll never lie to you, Katie. You know how I feel about lying. So you know I'm telling the truth when I say I love you more than I've ever loved anything."

His mouth came down on mine, gently coaxing at first, then turning rougher when I responded. My lips tugged up against his as joy obliterated the last of my grief. As his tongue plundered my mouth, I melted for him, and I knew he had well and truly mastered my body and my heart. One day, I would be able to tell him that properly. But for now, a ring and a collar would do.

# Epilogue

## *Reed*

## Three Weeks Later

Katie's pale skin was stunning, contrasting beautifully with the slim black collar that encircled her throat. She practically glowed in the dim light of the private room at Decadence, my favorite New York BDSM club. The owner had reserved this room for us at my request. With its stone wall façade and grey tiled floor, it was meant to resemble a dungeon. I had chosen it because it was a close semblance to Frank's basement, including the bondage apparatuses.

I could feel her fear quivering off her. It got the feral part of me hard, but my more savage desires were tempered by concern. I was intentionally calling forth her fear so that I could eradicate it, but watching her growing terror didn't please me in any way. Erotic trepidation was one thing; true horror was another.

Her arms were chained above her, pulling her body taut so that she was forced up onto the balls of her feet. Despite her fear, she still looked sexy as hell stretched out for me like that, vulnerable to whatever I wanted to do to her. In this position, her fate was entirely dependent upon my whims. She had to trust that I wouldn't do anything to truly hurt her. She had to trust me completely. I got off on my power over her, but I loved her for that trust.

As much as I loved her, I still needed something more from her. I needed it *because* I loved her. It was an essential part of me that needed to be fulfilled, and I knew she wanted to give it to me.

She was just scared. I had allowed her the time I promised her, but it had been long enough. She was still haunted by what had happened in that basement, so I was going to replace those memories with something more powerful.

I brushed her hair off her shoulders, and she jolted at the light contact. It wasn't a pleasurable little jump. I suppressed the urge to growl out my anger at the man who had done this to her. My anger wouldn't help her now.

*Control.* I took a deep breath and found it again.

I slipped the blindfold over her eyes. The chains rattled over her low whine.

"Reed, please don't. I don't want this."

The sound of her distress almost broke my resolve. Almost. "We've talked about lying, Katie. You're lying to both of us right now. I know how hard you come when I tie you up and blindfold you. You're letting something ugly get in the way of what you want. And I won't tolerate that."

I pressed my chest to her back, and my hands found her breasts. Despite her protests, her nipples were peaked and ready for my torment. I pinched them to remind her of who was in charge. The way her hips rolled against me as she squirmed made my cock strain against my leathers. I wanted to free myself and plunge into her wet heat right then, but she wasn't ready for that yet. There was more I needed to do to make her forget she had ever been afraid of what we shared.

I nipped at her earlobe, enjoying the way she shivered in response. "I'm going to hurt you, Katie." She stiffened, and I pinched her nipples again to call her back to me. The pain I gave her tied us together. She needed the release it gave her, and I needed to see her complete abandon under my hands. Until she accepted that she longed for it, there would always be a barrier between us. "I'm going to hurt you, and you're going to accept it. You're going to enjoy it. And then you'll thank me for it. You'll thank your Master for giving you what you need."

"Reed, I…" Her voice wavered. "I don't think I can."

I continued to tease and torment her nipples, distracting her from her worries. Her head dropped back against my shoulder. "I know you can." My hand skimmed down over her abdomen and dipped between her legs. The wetness I found there satisfied me on a soul-deep level. Her body knew what she wanted, even if her mind hadn't yet been convinced.

Well, I would just have to convince her. I knew just how to break her down, and the sweet spot between her legs was a good place to start. I found her hardened clit and traced slow, teasing circles around it. She rocked her hips up into my touch, seeking more. I pinched the little bud in response to her efforts. I couldn't hold in my low, satisfied chuckle when she cried out. I loved watching her come apart under my touch.

Again, I restrained myself from going further. I had promised her pain, and I hadn't even begun to give it to her. Her little whimper of protest when I pulled away brought out my slightly evil smirk. Denying myself was worth it when I got to enjoy how much my denial affected her. She needed me just as badly as I needed her, and that was immensely gratifying. No, it was more than gratifying; it was vital.

I retrieved a cane from my kit bag. It was harsher than anything I had used on her before, but she would need more pain than usual in order to work through this.

She shifted her weight nervously as she waited for what I had planned for her. I took it as an excuse to begin. The cane whipped through the air and came down on her ass with a satisfying *thwack.*

"Be still," I admonished over her shocked shout. She stopped shifting instantly. All her muscles went rigid, and she stopped breathing.

My hand stroked down her back in reward. She shuddered and sighed, and I smiled at the first signs of surrender.

I began a series of light taps of the cane on her ass, working my way from the upper curve down to her thighs. Her lovely skin flushed a gorgeous shade of pink, and her muscles loosened as she eased into the sensation. Just as her head began to fall forward with her relaxation, I brought the cane down hard, giving her three hits in quick succession. Horizontal red lines bloomed across her soft flesh, and she let out a harsh cry.

I stroked her back again, soothing her until her breathing returned to a normal rhythm. I resumed the light taps, but this time her tension remained as she anticipated the next hit. So I gave it to her. *One, two, three, four, five.*

She screamed and arched away from me. I resumed tapping immediately, not stopping to comfort her with my hand.

When her muscles relaxed this time, it was in acceptance. She ceded to my control over her body, surrendered to the pain. I gave her one last hit, and her head bowed with a gasp. When I reached between her legs, I found her soaking wet and swollen with need. She moaned when I tested her arousal.

"Do you have something you want to say to me?" I prompted in my darkest voice.

"Thank you," she whispered.

I slapped her pussy. "Try again."

"Master!" She cried out my name. "Thank you, Master."

"Good girl." I thrust two fingers into her and found her g-spot. I relished her little shriek of pleasure as she began to contract around me, primed for her orgasm by the release the pain had brought her.

"Thank you, Master," she panted out as she came down.

I growled out my satisfaction and freed myself from my leathers. Denying myself for so long had made me painfully hard, but it was a small price to pay for what I had earned from her.

I drove into her fully, forcing her up onto her toes with the harshness of my entry. She fluttered around me, already on the edge of another orgasm. She fit me perfectly, in every way. As I began to move within her, I teased her clit with one hand while I tweaked her nipples with the other.

She exploded again, and her pleasure brought about my own. I rode her savagely as I emptied myself into her tight heat. My arms tightened around her waist, holding her up so that the cuffs didn't bite into her wrists when her body sagged against me, sated and satisfied. My breaths came in harsh gasps that teased through her hair, making the coppery strands float before my eyes. I was just as caught up in her as she was in me.

Her head turned, her lips blindly seeking mine. "I love you, Katie," I murmured against them before I claimed her mouth. I kissed her long and deep, until she quivered in my arms, her body heating up for me again.

When I finally pulled away to allow her the chance to breathe, she said the sweetest words I had ever heard. "I love you, Master."

## The End

**Want to know more about Kathleen and Frank's twisted relationship?  Check out their story in *Mentor*.**

A beautiful, nameless man took me. He wants to break me and make me his. He treats me like his plaything, but I suspect I mean more to him than idle amusement. The monster needs me.

What's truly terrifying is that I'm coming to need him. He sets my body on fire, and I crave his touch.

When trapped in the dark, the blacker shades of lust can be confused with love...

## Excerpt

## Prologue
### *The Mentor*

## April 20, 1978

I slinked further into the shadows, concealing myself in the darker shades of night.  The tremor in my hands came not from apprehension or hesitancy, but from anticipation.

I waited for my victim.

Soon, the darkness within me would be released, the pressure siphoned off.  She would take my darkness.  I would impart it to her, inflict it upon her.

I would be able to breathe again.

Seeking to still my shaking, I immersed myself in the memory of the first and only time the enigmatic pressure within me had been released.

*Screams.  Blood.  Death.*
*Power.  Freedom.  Absolution.*

I realized now that I hadn't really been alive before the day the light left my father's eyes. His lifeblood spilled over my hands, and the dulling film of perpetual apathy that coated my psyche dissipated. The world became sharp, my senses impossibly heightened. It was the closest thing to human emotion I had ever experienced. The pleasure that flooded me was the nearest approximation I could imagine to what normal people called joy.

But now the memory of that hyper-awareness – that sensation of being *alive* – tormented me as much as it pleased me.

No sooner had I disposed of my father's body than the sensation began to fade, and the dim monotony of my detached existence began to seep back into me. Now that I was aware of it, the dimness built, gathering slowly into darkness. My darkness.

It coiled within me, slithering through my veins and rendering my very pulse sluggish. It would overcome me, would consume me from the inside out, if it didn't find release.

Killing again wasn't an option. I might not have a formal education, but I wasn't stupid. I wasn't going to leave a trail of bodies behind and risk being caught.

If I kept *her* with me, she could take my darkness regularly. I would allow it to consume her rather than me. I would train her to like it. Otherwise, my darkness would devour her completely, and I would have to find a new toy. I couldn't risk drawing attention to myself by taking more than one woman.

Kathleen Marie White wasn't special to me in any way. No one was special to me. I had chosen her because she was convenient and she suited my needs.

Like me, she practically lived at the Hesburgh Libraries at the University of Notre Dame. She had come here to study for the last four years, and even though I was a few years younger than she, I had been coming here for much longer than that.

I wasn't a student, but I had always found solace at the library. The desire to avoid my father and my disinterest in mundane human interactions made it an ideal place for me to hide out. People couldn't speak in the library. The pointless tedium of social pretentiousness was muffled within those walls.

As always, she was the last to leave the library on a Saturday night. The light of the streetlamp near the entrance caught the reddish facets of her dark hair, crowning her head with a crimson halo for the space of a moment.

My mind conjured up images of how I might draw that blood red shade from her body in other ways. Something unfamiliar stirred low in my gut in response, and my pulse jumped past its normal tempo.

*Interesting.*

I had intended to use sexual torment against her. Sex held little appeal for me; it would simply be a means to an end. But in that moment, I understood its allure. When used as a weapon, sex might be pleasurable. The sudden stiffening of my cock told me as much.

I clenched my fingers into hard fists, willing their increased trembling to stop.

Control.

*Control yourself. Control the darkness.*

Soon, I would control *her*, and the darkness would never rule me again. I would be alive. More than that, I would revel in the heady power I had experienced as my father's life slipped away under my hands. She would give that to me daily.

She turned from locking the library doors, and I caught sight of her face. It was lovelier than I had realized. She wasn't perfect by conventional standards, but the hint of a contented smile that played around the corners of her mouth gave off a sense of innocence that was undeniably appealing. Her deep green eyes were large, only further lending to that vision of purity.

When I had watched her over the last four years, her beauty had been obscured by unconscious nervous habits. Usually, a small furrow persisted between her brows as she bent over a book, and her full lips were thinned while she chewed at a pencil.

I had chosen her for that very reason. Drive and determination were evident in every line of her body as she studied furiously every day. She thought she could shape her own destiny if she just worked hard enough.

But her fate was no longer hers to govern. What she surely considered her greatest assets – her tenacity and intellect – were the very qualities which would lead to her ruination at my hands.

There would have been no satisfaction in breaking a weak woman. Kathleen Marie White was exactly what I needed.

No, it was more than that.  More than need.

*Want.*

I wanted something.  The realization was jarring, the sensation utterly new.  My lips curled upward in a semblance of a smile, and my hand was rock steady as I reached into my pocket to retrieve the ether-soaked rag.

I would take what I wanted.

**Mentor is now available!**

# Want to know what happened to Carl Martel? Check out Lydia and Smith's story in *Knight!*

Abducted. Drugged. Broken. I became a plaything, a possession. If I did ever have a name, I don't remember it now. Slaves don't have names.

My new Master stole me away from the man who tormented me. He saved me and took me for himself. I've found my salvation in his obsession, my freedom in his captivity.

Will his brand of rescue leave me more broken than ever?

## Excerpt

I used to think pain wasn't real. At least, not in the sense of being a tangible thing. It was just the result of my primal brain's in-built response to inform me that damage was being inflicted on my body. If I trusted the person who was giving me pain, then I knew he wasn't going to damage me. If I understood my pain, it stopped being something to fear and became something... interesting. I could master the hurt and ride the high of the adrenaline that flooded my system. I could enter subspace, that gloriously blank place where nothing existed but the sweet endorphins released by the pain that I embraced.

But then He came along and turned that all on its head. He enjoyed administering pain to torture, not to pleasure. And I couldn't trust Him not to inflict damage. He claimed He didn't like it when I forced Him to damage me; He didn't want to mar his property. But that didn't mean He wasn't willing to do so in order to get what He wanted.

I had tried to fight the pain for so long, to hold on to my conviction that it wasn't real. It couldn't hurt me if I didn't let it.

But He gave me so much that it overwhelmed me, claiming all of my senses until my whole world was agony. I was perpetually trapped in some twisted, inverted form of subspace where nothing existed but the pain, but it gave me no pleasure.

My only reprieve was the sweet reward that came with the merciful sting of a needle. If I was good, if I obeyed and screamed prettily enough, then He would give me my reward. I lived for it; that was the only time I *was* alive.

But I had become so dependent on it that now the denial of my reward was just as terrible as the agony He gave me. It had been so long since I had gotten my last fix.

Tonight, Master was testing me. He wanted to see just how obedient I was. He wanted the satisfaction of seeing just how thoroughly He had broken me.

I was broken. And I didn't even care. All I cared about was my reward. Right now, my need for it was so acute that my insides were twisting and my skin was on fire. I was desperate to give Him whatever He wanted so I could get my fix. If He hadn't ordered me to stand in the corner quietly and wait for Him to return, then I would have been curled up on the floor sobbing.

But I wasn't ensconced in the stark loneliness of the pitch black dungeon that had become my home, and I didn't have the luxury of going to pieces. His order for my silence denied me even the right to voice my agony. He had brought me out in public for the first time, and I recognized the place where He had brought me as a BDSM club. He would be able to torment me here in front of dozens of strangers, and no one would stop Him.

The thought of shouting out a safe word or screaming for help didn't even cross my mind. All I could think about was when He would come back and doing my best to please Him so that He would grant me my reprieve. He had been gone for so long, and I was starting to panic.

And now a strange man was talking to me, threatening to hurt me if I didn't tell him my name. But I didn't have a name. If

I did ever have a name, I didn't remember it now.  I was a slave, and slaves don't have names.

**_Knight_ is now available!**

**Want to know more about Sharon, Reed's partner in the New York unit? Check out the story of her rocky romance with Derek Carter, owner of Decadence, in *Rogue!***

I've never been a failure. I don't allow myself to make mistakes. I've lived my life to painstaking perfection.

Until now.

I can't seem to get anything right. And when you work for the FBI, mistakes can cost lives.

Busting BDSM club Decadence for drug trafficking is my chance to prove myself. And no pushy Dominant is going to throw me off my game, not even sinfully sexy club owner Derek Carter. I have to keep him close in order to uncover his secrets, but keeping him close to my body while guarding my heart is proving more difficult than I ever imagined.

He might just be my biggest mistake yet.


## Excerpt

One corner of Derek's mouth ticked up as he turned his full attention back to me. With the bar at my back and his large body in front of me, I was struck by the sudden sensation of being trapped. He was so close that the heat of him teased across my skin. I shifted my weight on my stool, angling my body away from his in a futile attempt to escape that intoxicating warmth. His twisted smile became more pronounced.

"I don't appreciate being labelled as creepy, but I'll easily admit that I've acted like a total ass. Can I buy you a drink to begin to make it up to you? I really can play nice. If that's what you want."

The playful spark in his eyes held a darker edge. That lustful light let me know that he would rather not play *nice* when it came to me. And damn it if that knowledge didn't make an answering darkness coil deep within me.

*"As a Dominant, he's a master manipulator. He won't need to knock you down to get you flat on your back."* Smith's warning skimmed across my mind, but it didn't fully douse the unhealthy heat inside me.

*Careful, Silverman.*

"You're being creepy again," I pointed out lightly. "But I do appreciate a man who can admit when he's wrong."

He laughed, a rich, breathtaking sound. It illuminated his features, wiping away any traces of cocky amusement or frustrated ire. He looked... free. His melted caramel eyes were golden and almost boyish in their genuine humor.

"You're a bit of an ass yourself, you know," he informed me when his laughter died down to a chuckle. "Most people aren't so brazenly impolite, even if the person they're talking to hasn't been so nice."

I shrugged, but I couldn't hold back my smile; his pleasure was infectious. I might have been offended if it weren't for the fact that he was right: I had been acting like an ass. If the accusation had come from Smith, he would have earned himself a slap. But from Derek, it wasn't an accusation so much as playful banter. He made the insult sound like an admiring compliment.

"I prefer the term 'blunt,'" I told him with a grin. "Maybe even 'ballsy,' if you want to be crass about it."

"Oh, I can be crass, babe. I like to talk dirty." He winked at me.

"Creep." My pointed allegation was ruined by my amused smile.

"Damn." He smothered his own smile, doing his best to school his expression into something contrite. "I promise I can be good."

His attempt at wide-eyed innocence didn't suit him at all. He looked so ridiculous that I couldn't hold back my laugh, ruining his efforts to keep a straight face.

"Well, if you promise to behave yourself, I guess I will take that drink."

"I wouldn't make that promise to anyone else. But I'll make an exception in your case, as a form of penance. Which is something else I don't do, by the way." He eyed me carefully. "Maybe Clara's right. Maybe you will make a good Domme."

The way the lines of his face drew downward let me know that the thought didn't please him.

I did my best to ignore my unease at having disappointed him. I didn't like disappointing people. It was a reflexive thing, an ingrained response from years spent trying to please my father.

Shaking it off, I grasped at the opportunity to further my mission.

"That's actually why I came back," I said quickly. "I wanted to talk to you about what it takes to be a Dominant. Even though you pissed me off, you seem to know what you're talking about, and I want to do this right. *Safe, Sane, Consensual,* right? It's my job to uphold that." My lips took on a wry twist as I added, "No matter how creepy my instructor is."

Derek's brows rose in disbelief. "You want to sub for me to learn how to be a good Domme?"

"Maybe," I hedged, my fears getting the best of me. I knew I should accept immediately, but nerves made me shy away from the commitment. "I'd like to talk about it more before making up my mind about that," I amended.

He considered me carefully for a moment. Did he approve of what he saw?

*Stop that!* My entrenched people pleasing would get me into trouble here if I didn't focus on holding my own around this man.

Finally, he nodded, and I let out the breath I didn't know I was holding.

"Okay. We can talk about it over that drink and then revisit my proposal. What's your poison?" That signature smolder that Clara had warned me about threatened to make me melt for him at the mention of his *proposal.*

*Submitting to him.* Shit, I needed a drink.

**Rogue is now available!**

# Also by Julia Sykes

**The *Impossible* Series**
*Impossible: The Original Trilogy (Monster, Traitor, and Avenger)*
*Savior*
*Rogue*
*Knight*
*Mentor*
*Master*

*Torn (Caught between the Billionaires) (The Complete Collection:
Lucas, Jonathan, The Choice, and Consequences)*

*Dark Grove Plantation (The Complete Collection)*

CPSIA information can be obtained at www.ICGtesting.com
Printed in the USA
LVOW13s1758080814

398226LV00009B/200/P

9 781500 302443